Words from the Woods

tales of mystery
and imagination

Fyling Hall

Text ©2018 Fyling Hall School

Words from the Woods tales of mystery and imagination

Published by Sunmakers
www.sunmakers.co.uk

Version 1.0

Designed and Edited by Ayd Instone.
Cover image: Hee Joo Jin

ISBN: 978-1-908693-26-6

www.fylinghall.org

To the next generation of writers and readers
and the authors and teachers who inspire them.

Contributors

Gabriela Adamczyk
Olivier Archer
Henry Atkinson
Isaac Atkinson
Anna-Luisa Ayckbourn
Eska Beeforth
Amber Beeforth-Miller
Clementine Bentley
Laura Blumoser
James Brine
Edward Burke
Carolina Clements
Jenna Coleman
Alan Davison
Ellie Dudley
Freddie Elson
Nuria Escoda
Anisia Fedotova
Callum Ferrer
Sophie Ferrer
Georgina Glaysher
Dominik Hansabut
Eve Harrison
Paula Hattenkerl
Annabel Head
Islay Hudson
Ayd Instone
Mabel Instone

Hee Joo Jin
Asa Jones
Damon Kelly
Suyean Kim
Manfred Kong
Asia Koter
Konrad Lüdecke
Maria Matschke
Rory McAdam
Milly McMorrow
Lily-May Newman
Christie Radford
Toby Richardson
Tomas Richardson
Archie Robinson
Phoebe Russell
Joseph Salt
Corbin Shearing
Alethea Shephard
Kieran Smith
Fran Sutterby
Maeve Sutterby
Silas Venus-Haslett
Calli Walsh
Lilli Walsh
Damilare Williams-Shires
Sonny Wilson
Ruby Wormald

Contents

Words used in this book

Welcome to The Intergalactic Writers' Guild

"The true weird tale has something more than secret murder, bloody bones, or a sheeted form clanking chains according to rule. A certain atmosphere of breathless ad unexplainable dread of outer, unknown forces must be present; and there must be a hint, expressed with a seriousness and portentousness becoming its subject, of that most terrible conception of the human brain - a malign and particular suspension or defeat of those fixed laws of Nature which are our only safeguard against the assaults of chaos and the daemons of unplumbed space." – H. P. Lovecraft, 1927.

I'd long had the goal of inspiring children to write more and better stories and collect them into an anthology. Initially it had the double goal of using stories with some students as a tool to better engage them in science, by encouraging them to create a narrative around a scientific phenomenon. With others there is a need to draw out the creativity of students already proficient in science but less likely to develop their imaginations. Surprisingly, most of the schools I had worked with had little interest in the idea. It was only when I came to Fyling Hall in January 2016 that I could set up an after-school club to develop these ideas and The Intergalactic Writers' Guild was born.

I say 'guild' and not 'club' as just like the trade guilds of old, the idea of the meetings was to develop, hone and improve our craft of storytelling. We met for an hour every week and played creativity games designed to encourage and develop different aspects of story creation and writing: imagination, description, characters, locations, voice, atmosphere, style and purpose. Two of these exercises resulted in short pieces that are so interesting, I've included them as works in their own right at the back of this book.

The themes we explored centred around two interesting techniques that you'll see reflected in most of these stories. The first and most powerful starting idea for a creative expression was the speculative fiction idea of 'what if?' - asking a question or changing one aspect of reality and dealing with the consequences which unfold as a story.

The other key theme was 'the ghost story' which was especially exhilarating during dark autumn and winter evenings (and sometimes telling stories by candlelight) and it is this genre more than any other which threw up so many interesting ideas. You'll find many of the stories herein fall into that category.

After one meeting of the Guild, one of the students suggested that we cannot set a ghost story in the present day as we have mobile phones and other technology that undermine the belief in the supernatural. In essence he was right; if you have a mobile phone you are able to call for help. In a ghost story there must be no help. The protagonist (and therefore the reader) must be alone and cut off from any advice, support or a way out. For the ghost story to work there must be, in the moment, no way to explain it or to rationalise it. M.R. James stated that a ghost story should be set in the near past, ('at the turn of the century' or 'just before the war' were examples he gave) but removed enough from the day to day of the moment to add to the believability and that things in the story are not quite as they are now. This is confused with us as twenty-first century readers of James, who sets all his stories in his own near past (the late Victorian era) which to us is long past. As with many of the great ghost writers from the gothic era to the First World War; Poe, Lovecraft, Henry James, Sheridan Le Fanu, Violet Hunt, and Dickens who all set their stories in the same era, one contemporary with their own time. Because of this we often mistake the ghost story as a Victorian phenomenon. For this reason I'm not too convinced the past is necessary for a ghost story to work as long as one incorporates the other values of the genre which you will find our writers have adopted here. The main one is, as Lovecraft describes above, that feeling of 'wrongness' which is generated in the unbeliever's atheistic mind. Many of M.R. James' protagonists are of this nature; unbelieving, rational, educated and practical men, who do not believe in ghosts and probably take a materialistic modern view of religion too. It is on these minds that the ghost story works best. In the text, the unbeliever is forced to cross the chasm of the unknown in a way they are not prepared to do, having nothing to fall back on, finding all their dearly held assumptions of the world falling short. The other attribute of a good ghost story is the idea of dreadful anticipation, that something or someone is coming, but with little knowledge about who, what or where such a visitation may come from or what it wants. Don't be surprised therefore at the breadth and depth of nightmarish horror that these young minds have channelled.

It is said that one should really live a full life of many different experiences before setting the pen to write. This is possibly true for the novel, but the short story allows such a concentration of ideas in a compact space that you'll be astonished that such young people could think such dark or deep thoughts. Imagined suffering, horror and terror seems to come very easy to our children's imagination: they know what scares them; it scares all of us. They are close to the fear of the unknown and here they have figured out how to channel and express it. In most of the stories, the writers have easily created alternative worlds, in the past, present or future and created an alter-ego protagonist that is not necessarily based upon themselves; don't assume a female writer's main protagonist is a girl and vice versa. Some of the stories reflect the writer's or the writer's generation's preoccupations, extrapolations of personal lives, hopes and fears. Some are based upon ideas learnt at school or shared recent history. The immense loss of wartime is a popular theme as is their concerns and worries about their futures. And be prepared: where there are ghosts, they are not nice to know. They will always bring a disturbing sense of foreboding; there is no 'Blithe Spirit' here, following closely James' formulae:

> *"Two ingredients most valuable in the concocting of a ghost story are, to me, the atmosphere and the nicely managed crescendo. ... Let us, then, be introduced to the actors in a placid way; let us see them going about their ordinary business, undisturbed by forebodings, pleased with their surroundings; and into this calm environment let the ominous thing put out its head, unobtrusively at first, and then more*

13

insistently, until it holds the stage. Another requisite, in my opinion, is that the ghost should be malevolent or odious: amiable and helpful apparitions are all very well in fairy tales or in local legends, but I have no use for them in a fictitious ghost story." – M.R. James, 1924

Not all contributions contained herein have come via the Guild. A batch of stories were written as part of English lessons for years 7, 8 and 9. Some being given themes such as 'the cold' or 'the other side'. I also gave two special sessions on 'Writing the Ghost Story' and on 'Speculative Fiction' for year 7 which have led to some fascinating stories that I was able to harvest and that you can read in this collection.

So what can you expect to find in this book? Most are self-contained short stories. Some are extracts from much longer planned stories. A few are poems. They are presented in no particular order. I have decided not to give children's ages in the book. There are contributions from those age 10 to 18. Some stories have been edited slightly for their inclusion here. Overall we have 58 contributors, including those who have submitted artwork from their GCSE portfolios (not linked to any of the tales) to break up the pages between stories. Special thanks goes to Hee Joo Jin who painted the original artwork for our cover and Head of English Alex Woodhead and Julia Jackson who proofread our grammar and punctuation.

The challenges that face young authors are the same that face any young person in any 21st century endeavour and fall into these four categories, which we aimed to deal with one by one in the Guild:

1. How to have an idea (*creativity*).
2. How to turn an idea into an interesting narrative (*communication skills*).
3. How to keep going (*perseverance and resilience*)
4. How to have a great ending *(finding purpose and meaning*).

These skills of **creativity, communication, perseverance and resilience** as well as finding **purpose and meaning in life and work** are critical for a rounded education and fulfilling life and yet they don't always fall within the traditional curriculum in many schools. For that reason I believe the work we have done here is of the highest value and has, I hope, enriched the experience of those that have participated in this book. On behalf of all our writers, artists and myself, we now hope that it will in some small way entertain, inform and educate you too.

Ayd Instone
Fyling Hall
April 2018

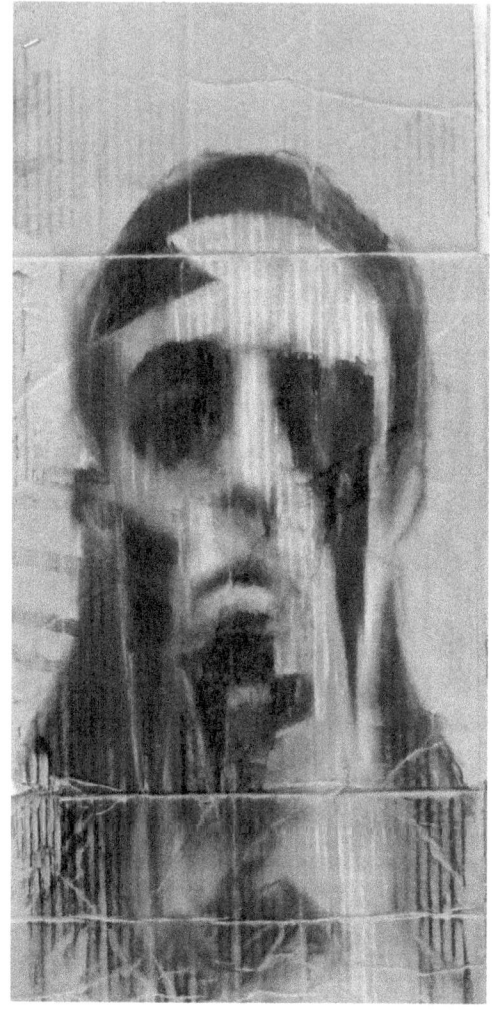

Suyean Kim

Shadows Amongst the Mountains

by Silas Venus-Haslett

There are many strange myths amongst the Himalayan Mountains. One of the lesser known stories concerns mysterious, tall, black figures who are said to inhabit the tallest, inaccessible mountain ridges. A number of deaths have been attributed to these 'shadow creatures' although no official sightings had been recorded. When a body could not be found, it was the name of the Shadow Creatures which was whispered under the breath.

This fascinated a certain mountaineer, who went by the name of Alexander Blake, who vowed to make his name by trying to discover these creatures, if they existed.

Blake loved to explore and was intrigued by the unknown with an insatiable desire to be the first or the best at anything he turned his hand to. He was as hot-headed as the mountains were cold, and ignoring advice from the Sherpas, he set off up the Himalayas alone.

Scouting out the mountains with his binoculars, he saw nothing unusual as far as the eye could see. For hours he searched until the light began to fade. Then Blake stumbled upon something that was very intriguing.

17

"Footprints?"

They were twice the size of any normal human feet and had no resemblance to any known organism on the planet. They had four triangular shapes; three at the front and one at the back. Blake examined them further and found that they led on down through the mountain. Making his way down, Blake took out his binoculars and once again examined the surrounding when his glasses settled upon a strange shadowy humanoid figure standing tall in the distance.

Blake froze. Not simply because of the icy winds against his face and snow beneath his feet, but in sheer shock and excitement. The thing turned around and descended behind the mountain.

"Fascinating!" Blake said under his breath. "So, the legends are true."

He quickly rummaged through his backpack looking for his camera and darted clumsily up the hill, hoping to snap a shot of the entity, but as he staggered to the top, the creature was gone, once again leaving the same strange footprints.

Nightfall was coming and as the sun went down, so did the temperature. A storm was coming. He set up his tent, cooked and ate a meal quickly, then laid out his sleeping bag and tried to snatch some sleep as the snow storm hit. As the night went on and the storm finally settled, strange things began to happen. Blake heard footsteps outside, crunching through the snow. They grew louder. As Blake woke, his fear turned to terror: he lay there, so very still, protected only by the thin canvas. He could sense many tall black shadow-like figures outside. He couldn't move: he did not want to. He held his breath. The fact that there were these mysterious entities on the other side of the thinly layered tent terrified Blake, but that wasn't what disturbed him the most; it was the whispering, the hissing and the mumbling, the unsettling noises these creatures made. Blake knew that the noise these beings were saying was to them, speech. Blake knew one thing. These creatures were not animals, but neither were they human. What were they saying? What were they going to do? What hideous thoughts were running through the minds of these Shadow Creatures?

Blake couldn't stand it any more. He grabbed his flashlight from out of his rucksack and charged out into the frosty wind, with the one thought of startling the creatures and making good his escape. But there was nothing outside, no-one. The entities had disappeared. There was only the mountain and the snow.

Morning came as the sun rose over the ridge. Blake had had no sleep. He had been crouched all night wondering if the Shadow Creatures would return. By now he had had enough of this place and perhaps witnessed all that he needed, all that he could. Blake packed his tent and equipment away and hoisted his pack onto his back. As he turned to head back down the mountainside, he found himself, to his horror, to be standing face-to-face with a solitary Shadow Creature. There it was, standing just a few feet away from him, staring right at him. The creature was horrifying, with long spindly arms and legs: its rib cage pushing out of its greyish-black body. Worst of all was its face. The creature had no nose and completely white eyes, emotionless and unsettling. Its mouth was crusty and cracked with rows of sharp, long teeth. Blake was more traumatised now than ever.

"What do you want from me?" he stuttered, staring at the horrifying figure.

The creature took a stride towards him. Blake sprinted off in the opposite direction, running as fast as he could, panting and panting, back up the mountain. As he turned around, the shadow creature began effortlessly picking up the pace and closed in on him. Breathlessly, Blake dashed up an icy path up to the tallest ridge and did not look back. He reached the summit and came to the edge of a sharp drop, a cliff edge leading off into a bottomless, icy crevasse. Blake trembled as he stared into the abyss. He turned around only to see the creature once again staring at him with those emotionless white eyes. Blake took a step back. Shards of ice crumbled away and tumbled silently into the crevasse. He was too petrified by the creature to focus on the instability of the mountain. The creature continued slowly striding towards him, its ghostly black hand stretched out for him with its hideous, bony fingers.

"Stay away from me!" Blake screamed, but before the creature could even touch him, the snow beneath his feet split off the mountains and he fell with it.

As Blake plunged down into the dark bottomless abyss, the last thing he saw was the Shadow Creature staring down at him, its hand still outstretched. He descended into the crevasse and disappeared into the darkness, to become another body swallowed by the mountains of the Shadow Creatures.

Silas Venus-Haslett

The Left Window

by Georgina Glaysher

I popped the bonnet of my dad's rusty car to examine the damage. As I clipped on the jump leads, Freddie came zooming at me at eightly miles an hour. While making tyre tracks over the newly planted grass, he dragged me closer and squealed.

"Come with me, they've finished it. THE ARCADE. IT'S FINALLY OPEN!"

I hopped on my chopper and followed him down the lane. Freddie snatched the large pot of pennies from the lemonade stand on the corner of the street. The year was 1981.

The arcade was only a block or so away, but you could see the blaring lights for miles with the animated sounds of Space Invaders and Pac Man. We parked our bikes under the large flashing sign, 'Radley Amusements'. I looked up and saw a grimy old window to the left of it. For a moment I thought I saw someone there, a girl, looking out. She looked odd, frightened. I looked again but there was no one there.

Freddie and I played all day until night fell on the small town. That night, the 18th November, I went to bed as usual, but could not get to sleep. As I finally drifted off, I jolted upright, freezing and dripping in cold sweat. As I pulled the duvet over my shoulders, I heard a sound that I had never heard before and never want to hear again. The sound was a troubled voice, like a young girl's wail, coming from the direction of the arcade. I convinced myself I was just tired. The next morning I went to school as usual and told Freddie what I thought had happened.

"Don't be ridiculous. Ghosts aren't real!" he said. But already the thought of searching the arcade was buzzing around my head.

I knew Freddie couldn't come with me. He'd been grounded for stealing his sister's pennies. So that night, I took my flashlight and nothing else. I prized the hinges off a window around the side of the building and climbed in. In front of me was an old staircase. At the top of the stairs, I found a long straight corridor, the walls covered in mouldy and cracked tiles. I must have been directly above the arcade. This floor mustn't have been refurbished yet. I entered a room with three baths aligned in the centre. Hanging on a tap was a cloth, dripping wet.

I continued on to another room on the right. My sneakers squeaked along the polished wooden floor. Five or six beds were crammed into this room. I heard a faint noise that sounded like the broken wheels of a medicine trolley coming from the corridor. It seemed to become louder and louder until a cold shiver struck down my spine as the door to the room slammed shut. The squeaking noise had stopped on the other side of the door. I tried the handle. The door was locked. Too frightened to call out, I ran over to the window. It was covered in grime. Looking down into the street below, I could just about make out a girl standing there, about my age, looking up at me, holding onto a chopper bike. I screamed.

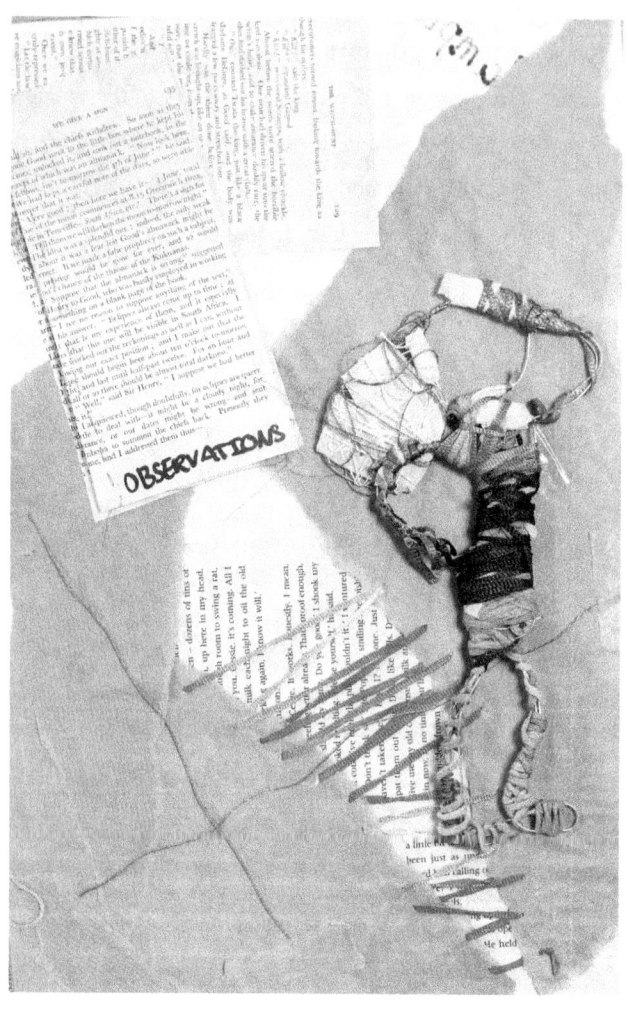

Silas Venus-Haslett

The Gravity Forecast

by Archie Robinson

Gravity. How do you tell what it will do, because, of course, it is always changing? This was exactly the question which Dr Teal had been trying to find out.

You see, gravity changes every day. One day it may be strong; the next it might be weak. There had been changes for about ninety three years, and the world had had to change quite dramatically since then. Once it started, scientists decided to measure it in percent. 100% was what gravity was before the changes, and anything below meant that things were lighter and anything above meant that they were heavier. The measuring of gravity had been difficult at first, often involving lots of weights and scales, but this had been hard. After a while, a man named Sarten Pike had made the 'Gravitational inference machine' or 'grav' for short.

Obviously the changes had made building and maintaining things a great challenge, as the structures would need to be strong but light. Advances in science, however, had made this task fairly easy. Mainly the use of graphene, an extremely strong and light material, had helped to overcome this hurdle, becoming cheap in large quantities, after a method to make it easily and affordably was discovered.

Dr Teal had been trying to find out a way to predict the way in which gravity would change for the past nine years (a kind of 'gravity forecast'), but it was proving to be difficult. He was looking at all of the old gravity readings, trying to spot any patterns, but there was nothing. He gave it one last check and then packed up his things. He opened the door and walked down the corridor. Everyone else had left the facility before the switch, which happened at midnight, but Teal had stayed. He was an important man in the faculty and got all of the equipment, information and funding that he needed. He checked the time. 11:47. He decided he would wait until the switch, instead of going straight home. He reached the end of the corridor and went out of the big graphene-composite doors. Ah fresh air, he thought, he had been in his lab for almost sixteen hours, studying the records.

Then, at exactly 12:00, he felt the change. He became much lighter. He checked his portable grav and it read 43%. It had been 114 for all of the previous day, so he was happy. Everyone enjoyed a low day.

He slept late that morning. He checked his clock and cursed himself. He should be in the lab right now not lounging around in bed, so straight to work he went, after, of course, putting on some decent clothes. Obviously they were his usual garb: a pair of black trousers, a plain white shirt, a clean pair of boots and a plain white lab coat.

He met Dr Malery on his way to the faculty: a hardworking woman, whom he often worked with. They exchanged brief conversation on the journey. Nothing much of importance. Teal wasn't really there anyway. He was within himself, letting his body go on auto mode while he thought of ways in which he could complete his work.

Meanwhile, somewhere in the Arctic Ocean, there was a boat containing several lost sailors, who were acting like people who had nothing left. Not even hope. This crew had been part of a team who were looking for an exploration boat, which was trying to find some lost building which was meant to contain something useful. The boat had become lost in the middle of the Arctic Ocean. They had found the vessel, but the people on board had frozen to death days ago. While half of the rescue crew were searching the boat, it began to shift. At first the people left on the rescue craft had thought it was just the waves, but then the whole thing started to angle its nose up and slip into the cold icy depths. Everybody had been inside.

Now those left from the team were floating about in the sea, after getting lost in a seemingly endless ocean, without any charts: they had relied mostly on satellite imaging, but that had broken and the mechanic had been on the other boat when it went down trying to see if the engines still worked.

They had sat for days, drifting wherever the wind and currents took them, not even bothering to turn on the engines; constantly looking for land. Then one of them shouted and pointed. There was land! And as they came closer they just about made out a smallish building.

They all decided that if anywhere was better, it was there. So they got into the lifeboats and rowed over. Soon they arrived at the gate of the building and found that it opened easily. Inside there was a large book with a metal cover on a large stand and lots of old, dusty things on tables. One of the people stepped forward and picked up the book. It was full of complicated numbers and symbols, which none of them understood, but they thought it looked useful so one of them put it into their bag. On one of the walls they found a map. They all looked at the map and then realised that it showed them the way out of the treacherous waters, which they had come through, and back to waters which they knew. They took their chart with them and went back aboard their ship.

Dr Teal was just looking out over the harbour, after another two weeks of not finding anything, except new levels of frustration, when he saw a beaten-up boat coming into one of the docking bays. It was the same boat which had gone missing three weeks ago, which was presumed to be destroyed. "Curious," he thought. Something drew him towards it. He pushed through the crowds of people questioning them and saw the crew of the vessel. They all looked dirty and tired and one of them had a bag which seemed to be very heavy; all the other ones had taken their bags off. The man saw him staring, took off the bag and pulled something out: a book of some sort. A very large one with a metal cover. The man handed it to him and said, "Found this in some building while we were lost. We think it's the one the exploration team were looking for. Full of numbers and stuff it is. I thought you might understand it being in that scientist coat and all, so you can keep it if you want."

Dr Teal took the book from his hands and looked at it. It must be important if it was found in such a strange place. After all, you wouldn't just put your average maths textbook in a building in the middle of the Arctic Ocean. He thanked the man and took the book home.

He put it down on his table, feeling the metal dig into his fingers, opened the first page and gasped...

Nobody saw Teal for days after that. Dr Malery was getting worried. She had gone to his house several times, but there had been nobody there. So she had continued all of his research for him. Eventually giving up on the records and moving onto studying the grantamasitheric equations. Most people at the facility, however, just carried on. Teal had never really had a booming social life and had little friends, so he wasn't dearly missed by many. The heads of department had been worried for a time, but had soon become more occupied with other things, as Malery had pretty much replaced him.

Then, one day, he appeared. He marched down the corridor to his lab with a book in his hand and pushed a list into Malery's hands, which contained several pieces of expensive kit and materials. She tried asking where he had been but he simply replied "working." As soon as Teal was in his lab he began collecting the materials he needed which were already there and then waited impatiently for Malery to come back with the other things he needed. Then he started ordering her about to "Give me this," or "hold this steady". He appeared to be making a machine of some sort, but for what purpose was still a mystery. After about an hour a sort of pyramid with a flat top with lots of coils poking out and a large pole with a ball of Santhium in it began to emerge from the pile of junk on his desk. He pushed the pole in between the coils and attached a single wire poking out of the side to a computer, then he told her to go away and abruptly shut the door.

The device was nearing completion. He had found out all that he needed to know from the book and it was just a matter of piecing it all together and building a machine. He spent the next few hours perfecting and tweaking the coils and internals of the machine. Finally, when it was ready, he dropped a piece of Zuplium into the tube and looked at the screen and the first gravity forecast since gravity first started changing read 11,347%...

The Puppet

by Tomas and Toby Richardson

Everyone is afraid of something. For some people it's spiders, for others clowns, but for me, it's puppets. The old ones are the worst, with their big wooden crosses and long strings…

One day I was out walking. I was heading for the old skip just on the corner of our street. It was only a small skip, but it usually had some good things I could salvage from it. On this particular day, I was looking for something I could play with. However, I couldn't find anything. On my way back, I noticed something odd; the house where old McDougal lived had gone, and in its place, was a small shop. But when I told my mum about the shop, she just said, "What are you on about, James? McDougal's house is still there; I can see him in it." She waved to McDougal and went to collect the washing. I looked out again and saw that Mum was right; there was just a normal house next door, not a shop. This gave me quite a scare, but I told myself that it was a trick of the light or something, and the shop could never have been there.

The very next day, a terrible shock fell upon the street. Mr McDougal had tragically died in suspicious circumstances.

His funeral took place a few weeks later at the cemetery. To get there, I had to pass his house. But as I walked past, the birds stopped singing. A deathly silence descended on the street. I also had the feeling that someone was watching me. I shrugged it off and carried on to the funeral.

At the funeral Mr McDougal's coffin was lowered into the grave. The ceremony started. I paid my respects and left. Yet when I got back to my street, the shop was there again. I approached it, curiosity getting the better of me. Just as I neared the door, it opened noiselessly. I entered, compelled by a strange force.

When my eyes adjusted to the gloom of the room, I saw rows of antique toys gathering dust in the dim light. Clockwork monkeys gazed at me with unblinking eyes, old tin soldiers stood to attention to an unknown general. On the counter sat a wooden puppet, its head slumped, and its wooden cross hanging over the edge. It had a striped top and a bow tie. It was raised above the other toys, almost as if it was their master. Behind the counter was a hunched figure with his back to me. He looked almost translucent. Out of the corner of my eye, I thought I saw the hint of a smile on the puppet's wooden face. Then, slowly, the figure turned around. There, staring back at me, were the white, empty eyes of Mr McDougal. I stumbled back from the dead man, felt for the door and fell through. As I fell, I saw the shop disappear, and in its place, Mr McDougal's house returned. I sprinted home. There was no point telling anyone; they would think I was deluded.

In fact, next morning, after a good night's sleep, I was even starting to believe that I was deluded, that what had happened yesterday had just been a dream. Until I saw the package. I picked it up and slowly opened it, hardly daring to look. Inside was a puppet, its wooden face looking back up at me. I threw the whole package into the bin and quickly walked away.

Later, when I was in my room, my light went out and something started banging on the window. I took out my torch and turned it on. The light cut through the darkness like a knife. I shone it on the window and walked forwards, looking through the glass. I saw, or thought I saw, the shine of polished wood in the moonlight. I turned around and tried to forget about it. But suddenly I felt a breeze. I spun round and saw that the window was open. I could have sworn it had been closed when I last checked. I went over to close it. Then I heard a knock on the door. In came my friend Jonathan; he had come for tea, I had forgotten about that.

"This is cool," he said, picking something up.

I turned, looked at him and yelled out in shock.

In front of me I saw the crumpled body of Jonathan lying on the floor and a slightly translucent boy playing with a wooden puppet. He looked at me with white empty eyes. Suddenly he thrust the puppet at me. I took it without thinking and felt myself fall to the ground.

When I rose up I felt light headed. I glanced in my mirror and screamed. Looking back at me were a pair of white eyes…

Jenna Coleman

Falling

by Callum Ferrer

Tears are frozen to my face. The single person tent I'm trapped in holds two people, me and the ghost person I was before all this. A zipper on the far side of the tent has broken and now leaves the gaping hole of a door open, exposing me to the biting wind and razor sharp snowflakes. Sunlight is blocked by immense blankets of dark, sombre clouds, and stained cotton balls, crashing and rumbling, charge towards my lonesome tent. The head and shoulders of the stone giant lying above the clouds look down upon me. It remains emotionless and silent, unmoved by the winds, the cold and my cries. It's a desolate land.

This was meant to be a simple mountain climb up Mt Ushba. It was entirely my wife's idea for our honeymoon; we married last week. Taylor always forces me to come on her little adventures that I would be much happier to look at the photos of rather than participate in. I wish had just put my foot down there and then. I'm desperate for any warmth, so I think back to my wedding day. To no avail. The only thing that replays in my mind is the wall of white that hit us, that pushed my wife just enough to fall off the side of the ladder we were using to cross over a large chasm. I still hear her scream, high pitched and piercing, lost in the ferocious wind. If I close my eyes, I hear her yelling for me. I can see her holding on to the edge of the ladder, her two fingered mitten slipping wildly. As she held on, she looked at me with glazed eyes and told me to cut the rope. If I didn't, we would all fall down the valley. If I did, she would die.

"No, I would rather go down with you than live with the thought of cutting the rope."

She said nothing, just looked at me, pulled her knife out and cut the rope. At this point, I forgot where I was and dived towards her, all thoughts of cold and starvation gone. My only intention was to save her. I can hear her ghostly last words: 'I love you, and I will miss you.' With snow clinging to her red puffy cheeks, she looked at me and let go. As I watched her fall, the cold slowly slipped back into my conscious. My hands were right in front of me and I couldn't feel them, but could almost see through them. My whole body was numb. I couldn't feel anything. Why us?

My tent collapsing wakes me up from my day dream, her hollow scream still piercing my ears. The storm has passed, the winds have died down. I crawl out of my tent to see four feet of snow all the way down the mountain. As I finally venture outside, the snow clambers up to my knees, like sub-zero powdered sugar. All that can be seen is the vast waste land that lies beneath me with pine trees scattered all along the base. With the forest thickening at the bottom, everything is covered in light snow, reflecting the glaring sun back towards the peak.

A sudden tremble in the ground sends my heart plummeting as I see a wall of frozen water crashing towards me. With all of my searching I must have moved too much and unsettled all that is at the top. It doesn't matter where our guide is now; there is nothing he can do to save me.

Crashing down the mountain is a white wave, screaming towards me. The wind from it is cold and sharp, catching my lungs. I have no other option, but to accept my fate. My tears, still frozen mid-fall, are joined by others. Numbness and adrenalin allow for my only focus to be on a single burning question, 'Why us?'

It hits and I am surrounded by ice. My body seizes up, and I am suspended, weightless, frozen... so, so cold.

Christie Radford

Elizabeth Rigby Missing

by Olivia Archer

"I knew her very well," I said to the detective in a solemn voice. "She was my best friend."

The detective, a man so large he barley fit his circumstances, scanned my room after my statement was given about my beautiful friend, Elizabeth Rigby. Tears started to prickle my eyes as he looked at a small minority of things I had left of Lizzie.

I plucked up the courage to ask him a question.

"Will you ever find her?"

"I don't know," he followed, sharply.

A chill started to consume my body, my face now blank. Gathering my thoughts, about Lizzie, I started to hyperventilate.

"What if she is dead?" I squealed, as large tears started to roll down my face. "She could be dead!" I screeched once again, only this time using all my energy. I blacked out…

When I was brought back to consciousness, the detective stood over me on my carpet.

"Everything will be fine miss."

I looked at him for a second then rapidly sprung up and shouted, "It will never be fine until you find her!"

"My team are doing everything they can," he responded boldly.

I could tell in his voice he was trying to keep it together. I collapsed back in a heap on the hard, wooden floor of my bedroom. The Detective knew I needed space, so he left.

Later on that night I looked at old pictures of me and Lizzie, one picture was when we went to the beach last summer break. We laid on two pink fluorescent matching towels, our skin browning with the UV rays from the sun. I remember that day as if it were yesterday. I remember we bought pink strawberry and raspberry ice creams to match our rosy, glowing pink towels. Then after we played beach ball on the radiant, soft sand that was full of crushed shells, that glistened in the sun. One of the best memories I have.

"I miss her," I said, so lost in thought.

Ever since we've been little I told her EVERYTHING. She knows my struggles and how I tick. In the depths of my despair I need her.

After my dwelling on our past glory, I checked the news. It read 'Elizabeth Rigby Missing' in bold Italics. I was sick of this, this situation. I fell asleep straight away, racking my brain for memories and haunted by that news headline.

I arise the following day to a depressed mother who puts on a contented face for her baby and a 'father figure' and another day without Lizzie.

For the next three years I didn't hear a peep from the detective. Then suddenly, out of the blue, I required to be interviewed by the detective and all of his team, just because Lizzie's case was taken back to court. Later in the week I had to give a statement about what I had said previously 3 years ago. At around 4pm, on a typical Thursday I went to the court room and I delivered my speech. I stood up on the podium to speak the identical words thart I said three years ago to the detective.

"I knew her very well; She was my best friend."

Before I could finish my verdict, a familiar voice occupied the room...

"Good afternoon Olivia," said Elizabeth.

Silas Venus-Haslett

The Sun Show

by Kieran Smith

D evinki awkwardly tip-toed across, past rows of seats as people moved their legs back so he could move. He was balancing human snacks with his hands, two bubbling cups of liquid with one hand and some puffy salty stuff in the other. Alankan was standing up waving at him with two pairs of dark shades in his hand. Devinki reached him and they both sat down. He passed one of the bubbling cups of liquid to Alankan.

"What is this?" he said as he put his nose to the rim. It smelt sweet and he could feel the rising bubbles splashing on his face.

"It's called Coca Cola." Devinki said slowly as he could not pronounce it very well. "It's what all humans used to drink, some even needed a constant supply of it. They found some hats that had bottles of these with straws attached."

"Really? It's so sweet how could anybody drink this on a daily basis?" Alankan said after he took a sip. "What is that weird tingling sensation in my mouth?"

"Oh that's the carbon dioxide." said Devinki.

"Odd, truly odd."

"Indeed, it was one of the only artefacts discovered on the

surface of Earth. Luckily they kept it in a huge vault, so it must have been valuable. It had some scary molecules in that recipe, I don't think they realised what they were doing to themselves by drinking it."

"And what is this?" asked Alankan as he pointed to the open carton of small white cloud shaped objects with yellow at the core.

"This is Pop-Corn," said Devinki, again pronouncing the strange words slowly.

"Pop-Corn," repeated Alankan. He reached across and popped one in his mouth. His facial expressions turned from disgust to confused then to pleasantly surprised. "Odd food these humans have," as he reached for a handful this time.

"Indeed," Devinki agreed as he started munching on the popcorn in handfuls as well.

"What else was found on Earth, then?" said Alankan.

"Well not much really. Most of it was dust and ash. With a few remnants of human habitation there, no other animals. High levels of toxic waste and radiation, dead pinions, oceans with no life forms. Even the air is unsafe for us."

"Do we know what happened?" Alankan asked again.

"Well it seems that the entire surface of the planet had been destroyed by some kind of war, but a war where they killed each other by making parts of the planet uninhabitable for each other. A sort of civil war if you will. From what we know humans were selfish beings and only cared about themselves as individuals or their local tribal group. It became a major evolutionary disadvantage to them to struggle to see themselves as a collective. We assume that these factions refused to cooperate for a common good and ended up destroying themselves as a result. They'd squandered resources and poisoned their sources of food, wiped out other animal life, decimating their food chains. In fairness they were once thought of as a very intelligent and industrious race that surpassed many challenges and has lived for thousands of years but clearly not enough to pass through the great filter. They made it to their local moon, but nowhere else."

"The show begins in 5 minutes. Doors are opening so please wear your glasses," the announcement boomed all across the hall.

Everyone almost in unison put on their protective shades and the steel doors clanged open revealing the bright white hot sun and just above them was the already scorched Earth. It wasn't blue and green anymore, it was beige. The craft safely orbited the spectacular show of the red Sun, solar prominences endlessly erupting from the surface.

"Are there any humans left? Did any of them leave?" asked Alankan

"No one knows," Davinki said with a grave face. "Maybe the humans were advanced enough to build transports that enabled people to live in space for advanced periods of time and they are out there somewhere searching for a new home. We've no records of any. Maybe none of them looked to the stars at all and were too busy fighting each other. No one has seen them or any sign of them for millennia."

"The show will begin in one minute."

Davinki and Alankan looked towards the baking Sun and the puny Earth: the Sun was flashing, flickering almost, and it looked as if it was about to burst. They were both well into the bowl of popcorn and sipping on their Coca Colas. Wearing their protective eyewear they were thoroughly enjoying themselves.

Without warning, the Sun made a blinding solar flare and then began to erupt and inflate into a larger ball of red flame as it fused helium together to produce a wall of fire rapidly moving towards the the Earth. The impact made a spectacular explosion, which brought a cheer from the crowd. Billions of years of history had drowned into a pool of fire. The flash vanished and the Earth was gone. The new larger Sun was no longer as bright, it had turned into an even darker red colour. The sky was darker so stars were now visible and Jupiter could be seen orbiting in the distance.

"It was ok," said Davinki. "I prefer supernovas."

"There's one due to happen in Gamma Crucis in around a hundred years," said Alankan, "We could go to that?"

The Beast

by Joseph Salt

People usually talk about the seven seas but not many people know about the eighth sea because none come back alive. They say the last thing you see is the twitching of electrocuted bodies, and the blue flames of the burning wreckage of your ship…

I woke up as usual at 7:30 am and straight away I knew something was wrong. Getting out of bed I dressed in my gown. Everything was eerily quiet. Even the skyscraper grand father clock stopped ticking. I went outside and was greeted by the frosty morning. I was wearing only my silk gown. The cold bite from the sea nearly knocked me over; the icy breeze shook through me. I found the rest of my village…

Dead on the shore with the scared expressions frozen on their faces. Then I saw it… a hideous beast as big as the old baker's house with wings of a dragon. I must be dreaming but it is not a dream, it is a nightmare and I can't wake up. Also it had a body of a kraken with tentacles of snakes that breathe fire. I pour water on the fire. It only makes the blaze stronger. At that moment I swore an oath to slay the beast of which I had only heard in fanciful stories. I stole a fishing ship, well it isn't really stealing after the entire owner is dead. I looked back at what was once my village but is now a pile of smouldering ash. Suddenly the water erupted like an underwater volcano. My heart leapt out of my chest. The next thing I know I am lying on the deck of my (not so) stolen ship with fire surrounding me, exactly what the sailors tell me is the last thing you see before it gets you. That's when I realised I was not outside but in a cave, a cave with a foul stench of fish. Not any fish, rotting fish. I grabbed a harpoon for protection: it turned to dust in my hand. I saw the sun which blinded me, I turned to the darkness of the cave, I want to leave but I knew the beast I had sworn to kill was in this awful territory.

In that moment I saw the horrific beast swimming towards me. Then it flew over me with its plane like wings, with all the speed and grace of an elephant wearing roller-skates. I calmly and slowly stepped out of the way. I shouldn't have been so cocky. As soon as I moved it sprayed blue flames at me like a cobra spraying venom. I let out a shriek of pain. Suddenly a bow and one arrow appeared in front of me. I had one shot.

As it lurched towards me I shot into his mouth. The arrow impaled his tongue. The bloodied body lay limp on the floor of the cave. I felt a huge rain drop of saliva...

Till the cows come home

by Maeve Sutterby

I remember when father used to take the cows home, and I would sit on the step by the house, waiting, waiting. I am sitting there now, waiting, waiting for the cows to come home. I chuckle to myself as I remember when mother would say "You'll be sat there 'til the cows come home!" Then, we'd laugh to ourselves for a minute or two before silence fell upon our home once again. When she would laugh with me, or with anyone else for that matter, she would always have a flicker of light in her eyes, like a candle. I could always tell if she put on a fake smile, because the light wasn't there. She loved it in the country, especially farms, and she had been brought up there so she insisted that I be too. It's not like I dislike the farm, it just gets boring after a while, looking after the animals day and night. It does get tough sometimes, with only a mother and father, but I don't mind not having a sister anymore, as she died of influenza when she was six months old. At least with a farm, we are in the countryside, unlike so many others who are in the city and are forced to flee. They say we're safe here from Hitler's bombs but to be perfectly honest, I don't know why this war has even begun. I'm only ten years old so my parents don't really tell me anything, just that 'I'm safe.'

Suddenly, I've been broken from my daydream as a man in a dapper suit is strolling up the path and towards the house.

"Hello?" I say, standing up.

"Hello, is your father in?" the man replies.

"No," I tell him "he's sorting out the cows in the top field."

"Oh, when are you expecting him back?"

"Why?" I say, getting more curious by the second.

"I have a letter for him, that's all."

"What about?" I ask.

"I don't know. It's from the War Office." I feel the blood drain from my face.

"The, the War Office?"

"Yes, son. That is what I said," he replies.

"Oh, sorry," I reply.

"It's fine," The man pulls a dazzling pocket watch from his waistcoat and stares at the face. "Well, I have to go now, but when he gets back could you give it to him?" He pulls the letter from his pocket and extends his arm towards me. I take the letter from his hand. "Make sure you give it to him."

"Okay, I will."

"Bye now."

The man turns on his heel and walks away. I immediately rip open the envelope and read:

'Dear Mr Byde, we are recruiting men to help fight the war against Hitler and to fight for king and country. We need fit and able bodied men to fight but we also need you. Your country is relying on you to defeat the Germans, so come and volunteer at your local recruitment office. You will be loved and honoured by all of Britain if you go to war, so join up today.

Yours faithfully, the War Office'

I feel tears well up in my eyes as I drop the letter on the ground. I stand up and run, away from the house, away from my problems. I find myself in the orchard at the bottom of the farm. I curl up in a ball, lean up against an apple tree and think, think that Dad could be killed in this blasted war, and that I'll never see him again. A twig snaps nearby, and my head whips around. Nothing there. Another twig snaps, closer this time. I jump to my feet as my eyes flit around the grassy floor. Eventually I find the source of the noises, as there is a small grey squirrel standing on its hind legs in front of me. My body instantly relaxes. It stays still for about five seconds before darting up a tree next to me. I think to myself 'At least its father doesn't have to go to war.' An image of horror flashes into my head. Mother and I are standing in the graveyard looking down at a simple grey headstone on the ground. It's Father's. I wake up from the daytime nightmare and I start to cry again. I sit under a tree, whimpering to myself until I gather the strength to go home.

When I arrive at the house, I immediately know something's wrong. I walk through the front door and see mother sitting at the table. I look at her hands and notice she is holding the letter, as if she is protecting it.

"Mother, where's Father?" I ask. I try to stop my voice wavering but I can't. She is looking at something in the distance and I can tell she's not paying attention.

"Hm?" she replies after a long pause.

"Where's father?" I ask again.

"He's right here, why don't you join us for tea?" she replies indicating a chair.

"Mother, there's nothing there,"

"Don't be silly, he's right here next to me!"

"Okay mother, I need to go now. Bye."

I turn to walk away but look at her once more.

"Bye then love," she says with a smile, but it's not real. It's a hollow smile, I can tell. There isn't the light in her eyes; it's as if the candle has been put out. Forever. I walk away again, pushing the thoughts out of my head. Through the back door and run, run to Ben's house down the road. I knock on the door and he answers it.

"Hey Joe!" he shouts, a little too enthusiastically.

"Hi Ben," I reply bluntly,

"How's the farm?"

"Oh, same old, same old,"

"Alright mate, what's up then?"

"I need to tell you mate, that's why I'm here. But not out here, I wanna be inside."

"Okay then? My mum won't mind. Come on in."

I walk inside and tell him everything, about mother, father, everything. He is the best friend I've had since I can remember and he understands when I tell him things. I wouldn't say he's fat, but he's not skinny either. Lean, that's what I'd call it. Yeah. He has brown hair and dazzling blue eyes, which kind of scare me a bit. Just how blue they are, it's weird.

A few hours later, I leave Ben's house and walk home. It's dark by seven so I'm walking home at dusk. It's quiet and there's no one around but me. I enter through the front door of my house silently, trying not to wake mother. Then I notice her sitting at the table still, clutching the note in her hands. She's still staring too, into the distance at god knows what. I help her get ready and get her into bed. I know she's stressed about father, but it's weird seeing her so lifeless. I get ready for bed and lie on top of my duvet looking at the ceiling. I am tired, but I can't get to sleep. I stare into the darkness for I don't know how long, but I eventually drift into a web of broken dreams and nightmares.

Seconds pass, minutes pass, hours pass, days pass, weeks pass, months pass and mother gets a bit better every day. But one day, another letter comes from the war office. Mother picks it up from the floor and neatly tears the envelope open. She sits down again and clenches it tightly. I take it from her hands and read:

'We are sending this letter to deliver the upsetting news that earlier today, Private Byde was found dead in No Man's Land. The body was recovered which confirmed our suspicions. He had been missing in action since 5th March and has now had a war burial. Yours sincerely, The War Office.'

That's all it says. Nothing else. We are alone once more, but for good this time. Never again will I hear him sing to me, as I did when I was a child. Never again will we joke about taking the cows home. Never again will I see him smile. Never again will I sit on his knee. Never again will he kiss me goodnight. Never again will I see him. Never again.

I remember when father used to take the cows home, and I would sit on the step by the house, waiting, waiting. I am sitting there now, waiting, waiting for the cows to come home, but I know they never will.

The Girl at the Stables

by Islay Hudson

As I walked to the stables, through the thick black fog, I thought I heard a noise behind me. As I turned I saw the horse bearing down on me, the horse reared, and as its hooves hit me I felt as if I was falling into darkness......

At the stables I went to, there was a rumour of a girl who had died in an accident. Noone ever talks about her, so none of the other girls know what happened.

One day, my friends and I decided to spend the night at the stables, because all the horses seemed agitated, and Katie (the owner of the stables) had said it might be a fox, so she suggested we stay. We slept in the barn, and as we stepped in through the door, we were hit by the sweet aroma of hay.

Just after we set up camp, Daisy said she was going to the loo. After a while we started to get worried, so I said I would go and check if she was alright. I climbed down from the bales, and walked over to the shower block, opened the door and went inside. But no one was in the toilet block or anywhere else in the building for that matter. I wondered if I had missed her, or if she was playing a joke on me, so

I thought nothing of it until I got back to the barn.

"Where is she?" asked one of my friends.

"I thought she had come back, she wasn't at the shower block," I replied.

"Well she's not here," said Mia, Daisy's sister.

"She might have gone to see the horses," someone suggested.

So we all went to look because no one wanted to go alone, but she wasn't with the horses, or in the tack room.

"She might have been homesick," said Mia, "and gone home."

We all went back to the barn, but all Daisy's belongings were still there. Her bag was half open, and I could see her phone and purse sticking out. Just as we all got comfortable again, a thick black fog fell on the yard. In minutes we couldn't even see our hands.

"What's going on?" squeaked Mia in a frightened voice.

A figure appeared through the fog.

"Daisy?" I called.

But the girl kept on walking towards us in that odd swaying way. When we were able to see her properly, we saw that it wasn't Daisy.

"Did anyone invite a friend?" no one replied.

The girl did not stop at the barn, she kept on going, out into the fields.

When the fog cleared I saw something on the ground. I went to look, and saw the thing was Daisy.

"Daisy?" I whispered.

Daisy groaned and opened her eyes.

"What happened?" I asked.

"As I walked to the stables I thought I heard a noise behind me, as I turned I saw the horse bearing down on me, the horse reared and as its hooves hit me I felt as if I was falling into darkness…"

Silas Venus-Haslett

Death's Game

by Lily-May Newman

Darkness. All around, there was darkness. Even the cold, powerful glow of the moon couldn't be seen through the thick blanket of cloud which lay so perfectly over the sky. Even the sharp blades of lightning struggled to slice their way down to the core of the Earth. It was nights like this that made the sound echo around the dusky hall; in the frivolous, old, misshaped house that the man called his home. The single sound of a young maiden. Not of her giggling. Not of her singing. Not even of her crying.

"BOUNCE... BOUNCE...BOUNCE..."

Just the sound of her bouncy ball, bouncing off the walls in her bibulous father's best parlour was the only thing that reflected around the depressing walls of the desolated house.

"BOUNCE... BOUNCE...BOUNCE..."

"I never wanted to hurt anyone: not Dorothy, not her mother, not anyone. The people in the village one hour away would call me things like vicious, heartless, diabolical, dangerous; I even heard of some calling me blood thirsty. But they didn't know me. They didn't know what I was really like. And that's okay and possibly quite convenient. Because if they had known, they would have called me worse. Much, much more...

My wife, Dorothy's mother, was the only thing I ever truly loved. She made even the darkest of days in this beastly, slushy, out-of-the-way, withered building light and worthwhile. Sometimes I can still see the beautiful memories, through the broken light that we created in the walls of this dismal chamber; but the majority were clouded and shrivelled because of her.

Dorothy was three when my wife 'passed on', and, at first, we coped. In fact, I thought we coped very well; until Dorothy started to ask questions. Questions about myself and her mother. Questions about her mother. Questions about her mother's death. Questions that should not have been asked. And well, I couldn't take it anymore. Not even the most expensive of bribes would silence her. The only time I would get some peace was when she would play with that wrenched bouncy ball her Aunt Penelope bought her one Christmas; and still, that carried a horrific BOUNCE with it, as she launched it at the walls in my best parlour. I used to get so frustrated with her, the little brat. The maligned vocabulary which would depart my mouth when addressing her after she had pushed it too far, which, of course she always did, was just barbaric.

And, still to this day, I don't regret the 'little' accident that took place between me and Dorothy; or me and Dorothy's mother for that matter. And, still to this day, I don't really think I miss Dorothy or her mother; it's just when I hear the sound of that bloody bouncy ball.

Which, even though they are well and truly gone, I still hear! I can always hear it! And you would! Yeah, if you were me you would know and you would hear it!"

"BOUNCE... BOUNCE... BOUNCE..."

"Guilt! Some say it was guilt. Others started saying that I was mentally ill! I wasn't of course but they took me. They took me away; they took me for a mad man. But, you go. You go and listen. Listen to what lives in them meaningless walls. You go see what lies beneath the phantom like shadows, which will follow you around every corner. And, you go to the parlour straight forward from the kitchen, on your left, and you will hear the only thing that keeps haunting me of her, of them..."

Darkness. All around, there was darkness. Even the cold powerful glow of the moon couldn't be seen through the thick blanket of cloud, which lay so perfectly over the sky. Even the sharp blades of lightning struggled to slice their way down to the core of the Earth. It was nights like this that made the sound echo around the dusky halls; in the frivolous, old, misshaped house the man called his home. The single sound of a young maiden. Not of her giggling. Not of her singing. Not even of her crying.

"BOUNCE... BOUNCE...BOUNCE..."

In the village, we would call him 'ill in the mind', a mad man, a fool. But, if you go to that old, beastly, slushy, out-of-the-way, withered building you will hear it. If you should go to the house, an hour down the road from the little fishing village, you will hear it.

Hear the sound of a young maiden. Not of her giggling. Not of her singing. Not even of her crying.

"BOUNCE...BOUNCE...BOUNCE..."

Georgina Glaysher

The Traveller

by Dominik Hansabut

At first I thought it was another dream but as I explored this ominous world I began to understand that it was another unexplored reality, another dimension maybe. I had no memory of how I ended up in such a dark and mysterious place. The first thing I noticed was that I could not touch anything. No matter which material the object was made out of I could not grab it. However I was unable to go through walls and doors. While being in this strange world I was often trapped in rooms and had to wait for someone to open the door for me. Sometimes I was trapped in a room for days but that did not bother me because I was unable to starve or die of thirst.

I was very curious. This attribute of mine was the reason why I got trapped so many times. I wanted to know more about this world. After my first year, of which I spent most of my time being locked in various rooms and houses, my curiosity was almost gone. I had learned that there is no possibility for me to go back home.

The people seem to be very nice and kind to each other. They like to throw big parties and spend as much time with each other as possible. Most of the people seem very intelligent and most of them have a scientific career. Once I visited a laboratory but didn't get very far because of the vast number of doors. This trip took me three weeks but I couldn't even get past the cafeteria. I was very eager to look at their labs because most of the conversations revolve around science and academic work. Nearly every conversation starts with a simple question such as "How was your day?" or "Did you hear what happened to Steve?". Within half an hour the questions become more and more scientific. After another hour most casual conversations turn into a heated debate. The topics of these debates are often physics related. It seems that most of the scientists are physicists.

It took me three years to establish a way to communicate with someone. At first I noticed that whenever I walk through someone they would notice it. Later I found out that they would feel cold. After several failed attempts of walking through several people I finally found a scientist who took notes of the cold feeling he had. I tried to contact him via Morse code which he noticed.

After encrypting my message he asked me if I could hear me. I signalled him by going through his body. From then on he tried to ask as many yes/no questions as possible.

Within a year he invented a machine which could measure anomalies in the air hence allowing me to communicate more easily. He presented his discoveries to the scientific community at the end of the year. Most of the scientists were very sceptical but by the end most of them were convinced that I was existing.

Many scientists didn't believe that I truly exist. Most of them argued that the machine was faulty. Within a few weeks the scientific community was split into two factions. The scientists fell out with each other. A majority left the facility. Most conversations had become not about science but about if I am real or just nonsense. After all the conflict I felt really tired. I searched for a comfortable spot and lay down. I fell asleep instantaneously.

At first I thought it was another dream but as I explored this ominous world I began to understand that it was another unexplored reality, another dimension maybe.

Jenna Coleman

Self Discovery

by Damilare Williams-Shires

You wear armour that is more crack and chink than plate. Yet every chink is a testament to and story of your own strength, the strength to get up and grow stronger and every crack is but a symptom of your growth and a path that traces around you and leads to your heart. A heart that you don't always want to beat but it will beat the pain. It will beat the doubt. It will beat the demons that take your voice and your face and tell you YOU'RE NOT GOOD ENOUGH! THEY DON'T LOVE YOU! You will beat them because within you are sparks, sparks from a piece of metal reacting with the air and world around you to create light and fire. A piece of metal that will be hammered into something truly great. A Light in someone else's world helping them find their face. A fire to forge someone else's armour and burn their own path and contributions in life. So go on your journey, grow, evolve, find your face, find the field where you can blossom, find your spot in the sky to shine, find your rolling stone cover. And if they won't give you a cover, then shoot one. If you can't find your field, plant one. And if you can't find a spot in the sky, then shine as bright as you can right here.

Jenna Coleman

The Intruder

by Corbin Shearing

He was a dog: a husky. He was a husky dog of a man. His smoky voice would fill the room quicker than his cigar smoke. He wasn't a heavy smoker, but he enjoyed the pastime. His life was simple, as was allowed in the nineteen-twenties. Life was good for him; women, music and money.

He sat in the back of the smoke filled room, suit all done up and hand on hat. His ageing face was dull and glum, but a strange pleasure was conveyed in his slanted smile. The stubble of his face was stroked by his bulky hand, before it slipped down into the case. Smoothly, he lifted his saxophone from the silk coated case. Gently, he teased it to his lips and wavered for a moment. Putting out his cigar he stepped up and off his seat, placing his hat onto his head.

Taking centre stage the grey haired man placed the sax to his lips and let the magic unfold. The flowing water-like tune flooded the room. The soft and gentle tone soothed the ears of those nearby into an aromatic sense. He had a bulky body, but it was, like his music, naturally easy. He was pleasant to the eyes as his music was pleasant to the ears. He let the music take control and he felt the sweet release and freedom he only felt when playing in his element.

A girl watched him with glistening eyes as he moved carefully and slowly in rhythm. Her young, scarlet lips and golden hair and green eyes were sharp and inquisitive. She adored his music, she adored this place. Her sweet rosy red cheeks fluttered as he hit the good notes. She felt shivers down her spine as she became immersed in the moment. Her slender body curled in on herself as the other men approached. She wasn't here for them; she was here for the music.

When his piece was done he moved from the stage and floated over to the case and his empty glass. He sank into his seat and enclosed his instrument to its case. He clicked the box shut and sat upright to view his glass. It was empty, but it was alright; he had the money for another.

Gathering his soul, he meandered around joyous people to a bar stool. "Some of your best whiskey on the rocks, if you please," his voice, like his music, was calm, controlled and smooth. His voice had inner rust to it; whiskey-cured. The barman prepped his drink and delivered it before him. "Thank you," he trailed off to his drink.

She pulled into herself and rose up, sliding towards the musician at the bar, taking a seat beside him. He looked half-heartedly at her and she glimmered to him. "Hey, I like your music." Her voice was vibrant and upbeat, it shocked him a little, but the liquor drowned out the notice. He took another elongated sip and he lived the adored feeling of it running down his throat once again. The warm burn cooled his throat and lulled him into a state of bliss. "Man of taste, eh?" she joked around him, lighting her cigarette and offering him the lighter. He coolly pushed his hand into his upper suit pocket and took out a cigar. She lit it.

The two of them could feel a kind of tension between them, one that neither could name. He puffed out a long chain of smoke and glumly laughed to himself. "I ain't seen you round here before," he turned to face the bar, almost as if not bothered at her colourful presence. She flustered and also turned to face the bar and not him.

"I'm travelin' right now. Experiencing the culture of our time before it fades away. Maybe not in our lifetime, but hey, who's to judge?" Her lively face turned to him, as another side to her was revealed. "You probably think that I'm just another one of those girls who come out to smoky bars to enjoy some masculine company, get drunk and have sex – but I ain't one of them types - believe me or not, I'm an educated and cultural girl. I live for the sensations of the mind, not the body."

He guffawed. "I don't. Not for one second do I believe a single word that comes from your red lips. If you're tellin' me the truth, shouldn't you be at some kinda monastery, preaching about Jesus and his love for all of us."

"Yeah," she laughed, "I'm a nun because you don't think women can be logical in these times. Well, I got news for you - we are." He laughed straight back at her. His face was displeased and his body was tense. His voice turned into a low grumble.

"If you just came here to ruin a man's night, then please be so kind as to walk away now." She knew he wasn't sharing a joke with her anymore. The sax man's eyes were dark and tired the kind that could easily break into an untampered rage.

"No, I came here because I thought that you could understand and listen and not be like every other man in these smoke stained walls and in this smoke stained city." Their eyes met, both were ready to shoot when high noon came.

Tension was building as each of them stood down the other. He tightened his fist and clenched his jaw, placing down his drink and removing the cigar yet again from his mouth. She seemed to relax a little more, taking another sip from her own drink and letting out another rally of smoke from her mouth as her cigarette slung loosely in her hand by her waist. She knew what was coming next if she didn't leave, though she invited it. She just wanted to see how far this man would take it. Was he all talk, or did he really have something to back his words up.

"Hello there, or howdy, however you like it." A tall, skinny black haired man with a thick, black moustache came and slapped his hands on both their backs. His brown tweed jacket and his blue bow tie matched his clean white shirt and his dark grey trousers, strung up on braces. The man looked almost comical with his cowboy hat proudly born on his head. His face was beaming with a radiant smile that spelled trouble from a mile away. He looked late thirties, possibly early forties, definitely younger than the musician and older than the girl.

"Alright then, drinks are on me today. Or for the night,

whichever you want it to be, because it really don't matter no more." His flamboyant attitude ground the sax man's temper to a furious point. His night was going bad and the stranger would not improve it. "The name's Aldershot, Graham Aldershot, but you," he turned to the young woman, "you can call me Gray," his supposedly seductive tone just passed both his hearers ears as annoyingly boisterous. "So what's the topic of talk or do I think up one for us three?" The reply came as a non-existent no. They stayed silent.

"Actually, we were having a private talk. He's a well settled musician with a fair amount of money, but no time, you understand? I'm a start up player, I'm looking for some advice." She managed to remarkably think up the lie in a matter of awkward seconds. Her eyes darted menacingly at the intruder, but he pretended that he didn't see it.

"A musician? That's great! Although, I always struggled, I got this rare problem, can you help me?" His voice was pitched though it remained in the masculine bandwidth. "You see, one arm is longer than the other," he spread one arm across his chest and compared it to the other outwardly stretched arm. "I could never play the drums."

"You're a fool, Mister Aldershot. Now, if I could please get to talking with this young girl again, with your dismissal, it'd be much appreciated." He waved his hand as if to say goodbye, but Gray was still acting as if he didn't see or hear the man. He pulled a stool up and sat between the two of them.

"I know you're not a budding musician, so can we please forget that you ever lied to me?" He smiled cheaply at her and then at him.

75

His eyes glinted like jewels crowned under a snake's brow. "Don't worry fella, I trust you. But, you said you were a travelling woman, girl, whatever, yet you have the local accent, so please, less poker face, and let's all be honest for the evening." The older man couldn't help but feel that Aldershot's words were in some way a threat to the both of them. Unfortunately, he also recognised that he would not be leaving any time soon due to this man.

"So, I don't believe that anyone's really introduced myself here but me, so please, let's," the moment's silence was the resistance of the two cultured folk.

"Well," began the young girl, lifting her cigarette to her mouth, "I'm the girl and this man's the musician." The intruder burst out in an annoyingly fake and forced laugh. It caused a small scene, though he didn't care to notice that either.

"I don't seem to have made myself very clear. I've got a little friend in my pocket – I know what you're thinkin' girl but it ain't that. The musician's probably got the right idea."

"A piece of mind?" slurred the musician.

"Ha-ha, no… You're a funny guy, but no, it's a little friend that I like to call my third arm. A little powerful blast from my little finger and your brains, guts, blood, whatever I choose, goes everywhere. Do you get me now?"

"Unmistakably…" growled the grey-haired man with the depressive face and the dark eyes. He reached into his pocket and removed a cigar and a lighter, offering it to the third man.

"No, I don't, but I'm glad you've taken a small bit to me. Now, girl, what have you got to say?"

"What do you want with us? Can't you just leave us alone?" Her voice sounded broken as it stammered to compare to his light-hearted and almost scarily masked tone. He didn't care much for them; his attitude was playful – in a vile way.

"I want to talk, it gets awful lonely, y'know," he tried to act a victim, yet his act was bad, almost deliberately.

"You one of them mob members?" asked the built man, slipping himself another sip of his strong whiskey.

"Oh no, no, I ain't a gang man or whatever. I need money, sure thing, but never in such a brutal way. And you two just happen to seem like the richest people in this place. I'm sorry for that inconvenience." He smiled his cheap smile again and he called the barman over. He got his drink and he was pleased.

The three of them were at a loss for words, so they all took a thoughtful sip of their individual poison. "The rules are: you empty your wallets and give it to me; you don't scream; you don't make a scene; if you make a scene, I blow this place and add a little more smoke to the ambiance. Clear?" The two nodded silently.

"If we give you everything, we'll be fine; you can guarantee that, right?" Her voice shook, he could sense that she was trying to keep strong, but would fall utterly short of being brave. The intruder nodded, as they had, silently.

"Listen here, we can't give this man our money, you hear me?"

said the sax player to the girl when he thought the other man would not be listening as he called over to somebody else across the room.

"That's a stupid idea," she whispered back, noting the other man as he arose to greet the bald and bulky man that wandered across the room to him, "he'll kill us and take our money anyway. We can just give him the money and live to tell the cops what this man looked like, trust me about this." He shook his head solemnly. His soul seemed to depart from his body for a moment as he looked to loath the joyous man.

"I got me a better idea, baby doll; I got a nine millimetre in my sax case, if I can persuade him to let me get into it, then I can rip a hole in his leg and we can get the police to lock him up for a good long time." Her eyes widened and her mouth dropped.

"We can't do that, you can't just shoot a man, he has a whole life behind him, he ain't doing too good for himself and blowing his leg off ain't gonna help that," she hissed. He shrugged off her comment.

"I thought that you weren't like all those other girls. Sure thing, I was right not to believe you," he murmured. "What's there to live for anyway, but the pleasures off the flesh, eh? Prison ain't all that much worse than this, maybe less freedom, but that's only if we get arrested for self-defence, baby doll," he smiled weakly at her. It wasn't comforting to her, it was cold, and distant.

"Alright then, my friends," he burst out, "cash time," he whispered to them intensely. He held out his hands to them, open and wide.

"Sure thing, better than dyin' I guess…" grumbled the musician searching through his pocket. He handed over his wallet and Aldershot ran through it, gleaming at the money. The girl handed out her wallet and smiled in detest at his cheap grin. He ravished her wallet and his smile widened. The girl turned her head from him and looked down from the both of them.

"I was right, you people are loaded… Oh and what about that case you got there? Sax's sell for good money y'know." He showed his white teeth and put one hand out for the sax and the other into his coat pocket.

"As you wish," replied the sax player, slowly reaching down for his instrument. He frowned at the robber as the case moved inches away from the intruder. For the moments that the man kept the case from Aldershot's grasp, Aldershot frowned back.

"C'mon now, let's not make this any harder on either of us," he waved his hand in such a way that demanded the case. The musician stood up and kept his glum expression permanent.

"I don't think it could get tougher, mister Aldershot," commented the older man. Gray smiled without giving much heed of his words. His face fell to the floor with his body as the musician slammed the case into his face. Blood seeped from his nose and flooded his face and pooled on the floor. He crouched down next to him, signalling with his hands so that every man in the bar would not approach. "He's a thief, he was gonna take my life's belongings just then, call the police or ambulance, whatever... I'm leaving." He reached into the fallen man's pocket and removed his wallet, tossing the girl's money to her.

She sprang to the phone and called the police. The bulky man that had sent Aldershot down, stood up beside his limp body and began to walk out of the room. She rushed to their sides and lay down a cushion to comfort the robber's head. Reaching into his pocket she removed something else and pointed it at the leaving man. "Stop right there mister!"

"Baby doll, I'm leaving now, you should too," he turned around and his heart pumped as he saw the gun she was holding. "His little friend's your little friend too, huh," he chuckled to himself a little. He rolled his hat onto his grey head and smiled at the girl, "listen, your act is see-through... Ah, God... Money's all it now isn't it. Life's more than that, honey. You can put the gun back in his pocket and forget the truths said or acted upon tonight. You can start anew y'know. And if you don't, I was in my thirties and had brown hair with a parting to my left and a thin moustache. Thank you," he finished in his smoky voice with a gruff and rusted inner tone. His shape turned around and left the building into the dark night.

She slipped the gun back into Aldershot's coat and she took a big step back. Breathing heavily she could feel her heart pound against her chest. Feeling for her drink, she finished it in one quick gulp. It went straight to her head. Her blond hair fell to her shoulders and over her face as she stumbled across the room. Despite how weary she was, never had she been in more control.

"Honey," rasped Aldershot, holding his hand out to the girl. A hint of desperation was in his eyes. Slowly, she stepped towards him and knelt down beside him. Her eyes were wide and beautiful.

"Gray, this ain't gonna kill you - it ain't. Man up for me, yeah? You'll survive, as you always do," she finished her whisper to him as she kissed his unbloodied forehead. He smiled weakly at her.

"What are you talkin' about? C'mon, what is it, kiddo?" His voice seemed to drain in a state, which she showed care for, but not enough to sympathise.

Feeling the shiver that she felt earlier that night, she walked to the door, one foot before the next. Taking a glance behind her, the girl put an end to the life she had. "I'm a travellin' girl," she breathed gently to herself.

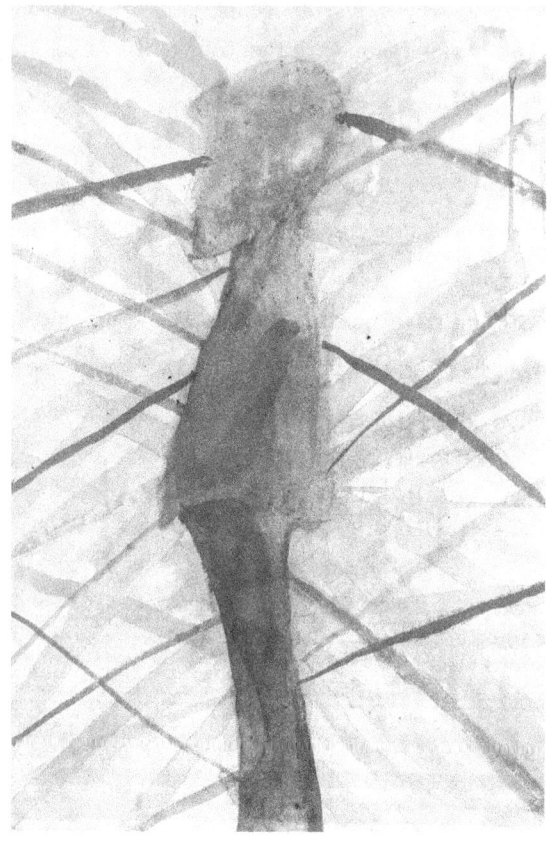

Jenna Coleman

Don't Look Down

by James Brine

"I wonder why that old lady didn't want us to buy this wardrobe," Mr Brown said.

"I know, it just fits perfectly and looks beautiful," said Mrs Brown as they stood in awe, gazing at their new, gold lined wardrobe, "and how lucky is it that a clothing store has set up outside," she added, still with a huge smile on her face, eyeing the store which was a storey below on the other side of the street.

The shop stretched out along the whole street and looked quite normal with green and red paint and gold trims. There was one strange thing about this shop, though. It took up half the street but there were no clothes on the racks and only one solitary mannequin. The tall standing man seemed to be looking up at them.

The following morning, Mrs Brown was just about to go to the shops, when Mr Brown called down, "Where is my work hat?"

Now being a business man, he did not like to lose his hat and he did not like what Mrs Brown said next. "I'm sure you put it in the new wardrobe, dear."

"I have already checked the wardrobe. I've got to go though."

On his way out he glanced out of the window and what he saw amazed him. The mannequin in the shop window was wearing his

83

hat. He was sure of it because it had the same personalised blue trim with the maroon leather on the brim.

Mr Brown was puzzled, unsure of himself, but he was a busy man and he had to be at work by nine o'clock promptly. He thought nothing more about the strange events of that morning.

That evening as he hurried home, past the shop, he felt a pair of eyes watching him, drilling in to the back of his head. But he was late, and Mrs Brown would be wondering were he was. He slammed the door behind him.

After supper, he went upstairs to look for his dressing gown, (he was a man of regular habits) but when he looked behind the door, all he could see was an empty peg glistening in the dim light.

"Oh, for goodness sake, where is my dressing gown!" Mr Brown yelled down to his wife, who dropped her tea in surprise.

"I thought you had donated it to the shop over the road."

"Wait, what?" he shouted angrily, as he drew back the curtain and peered into the gloom eyes stared back, almost singling him out. He saw the unmistakable blue, sheen of a night garment. A jacket? A dressing gown? covered the mannequin's shoulders.

And so, it continued. Day after day, night after night, Mr Brown's precious garments kept disappearing but still, seamlessly, the clothes reappeared on the mannequin which kept staring, almost keeping Mr Brown alone.

Now he only had his pants left.

"I can't go to work like this," Mr Brown screamed to his wife.

"One more night, I will have no clothes left, then what am I meant to do?" But then, instead of a response, he heard the draught coming in through the door, almost as if Mrs Brown had ignored him, or couldn't hear him. Then, again, he felt the eyes singling him out of the world, but now he felt, almost, a connection with the eyes, though not a human one.

Near the end of the day Mrs Brown seemed to become less responsive or was that just him being not loud enough? His skin was slowly growing paler but, was he just hallucinating? His joints were slower as well, almost as if they were made of plastic.

In the morning Mrs Brown rose up, looking for her husband, but she could not find him.

"Dear, dear, where are you?"

Then she looked out of the window, and to her horror, she saw two mannequins standing there with their eyes focused on her...

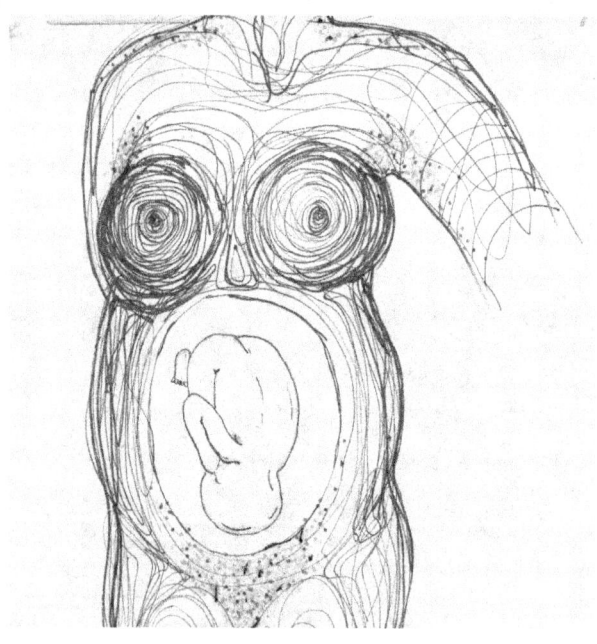

Maria Matschke

Isla

by Alethea Shephard

When we were younger we were inseparable. Her first daughter's name would be the same as mine. When we were younger the things we dreamt up were crazy like shopping in Paris or opening a café in Milan. These ideas were wild, especially with our background. We were different. We were the outcast of society, the unwanted, like the skin of a banana swept under a bin and left to rot. Isla Marie was my best friend and had been since we were children. We planned to grow old together. None of this will happen anymore.

Instead of me standing and reminiscing about our childhood all day I decided it was time. I stepped into the freezing water. It was up to my chest. Her colourless face lay there staring at me through the rippling water her skin like porcelain cold and hard with her deep blue eyes staring deep into my soul. Could I have stopped this. Should I have stopped her? Was there any sign of unhappiness or even her contemplating what she had just done?

I needed to get her home. I went to drag her cold bloated body out of the water but stood for a moment and let the water gently caress my burnt skin causing a bizarre numbness in my already bitter cold body.

In a moment I was laying out my deceased best friend on dew ridden grass. I stocked her face like some fine china way out of my budget. Then I remembered my lilac backpack which I knew had my hoodie in. I tore the bag open, retrieved it and gently laid it over her face. She wouldn't want anyone to see her in this way.

Then I made the call to her darling, doting parents who would do anything for their daughter. They were coming to pick us both up. Considering the situation they were reasonably calm over the phone, but they were not as calm when they arrived. Her mother took one look at her baby girl and dropped to her knees, sobbing hysterically. Her father tried to stay strong but he too shed tears. We took her frail, feeble body home. Her father and I laid her over the back seat of his tiny Vauxhall and we drove off along the rocky trail. I'd thought of how I should be planning her wedding not her funeral.

I thought you'd be on the end of the phone to me whenever and we would be meeting at our coffee shop in Milan, not delivering you wreaths at Christmas and birthdays and talking to your gravestone as I am now. You know you are my children's godmother. I know you and they will never meet. Oh my sweet Isla.

Sindy...Sindy

by Amber Beeforth-Miller

"Sindy, why don't you go out and play? We've been here three weeks now and you've yet to explore," her mother said practically shoving her out the door.

Sindy was a quiet and shy girl. Some said strange, that's why Sindy and her family had to move to the countryside. She would sit all alone with a hand on each side of her head rocking back and forth. London was no place for a girl like Sindy. She was always meant to be with me.

It was quite boring at first; watching her that is. Sindy would never question her mother's authority. She wouldn't say yes or no, she would just nod and walk out the door. Her mother repeated herself every night saying, "How about a little play outside, darling?" Each day Sindy came out to play, she looked a little happier.

Now, this was a chance for me to interfere. The next day Sindy ran home from school as usual but softly, softly I called her name, "Sindy... Sindy." before she knew it, she had come through the meadow as usual, and then stood at the top of the hill. Normally she went straight home, but not today. Sindy decided to stumble down the hill to the woodlands.

The young girl must have been walking for hours before she finally found my home, sweet home, an old world war two bunker. You see, about three years after the war, I had been playing with my twin sister also called Sindy, we were playing our favourite game, hide and "seek." It was her turn to seek so I went looking in the woods for a good hiding spot. After a while I found the bunker so I crawled inside and closed the hatch. I hung on the metal steps which led down to a very dark room with no natural light; when my sister Sindy hadn't found me I tried to open the hatch. But it was locked from the outside and I was never found.

But now I saw Sindy's body freeze-for just a split second-as she fell past me down that same bunker hole.

A Cat's Eye View

by Mabel Instone

H i everyone I'm Dandelion, but most people call me Dandy. It's cool being a cat. Oops I shouldn't have said that. You will all be wanting my beauty. Anyway, lets get back to my story. This is the story of the amazing, marvellous adventure of me.

I live with my pets: Susan, Michael, Lilly, Daisy, Oscar and Jacob. One day they all went out of the house (usually up to the hill to their school, but not this time). They started walking down the road instead of up. I followed them quietly, not being able to stand it any longer I yelled at them as loud as I could. At first no-one noticed me but then Jacob did and turned to see me.

I asked them where they were going as clear as I could (but perhaps all they heard was 'Meow!'). Lilly looked at me and shouted.

"Dandy! Come here Dandy!"

I looked at her and then ran down the road shouting, "I'm coming! Wait for me!"

So I followed them and then they turned a corner and I stopped short, not knowing whether I should go on. Then I heard them yelling and laughing on that lovely summers day.

I then suddenly made up my mind to run around that dreaded

corner and find them. I ran all the way round and saw them walking all over a farm. I ran after them, but a massive tractor got in the way. Their voices died away and I watched them go out of sight. I sat down and waited and waited for them to come back. They didn't come so I ran home as fast as I could. I shouted at the door but my pets didn't open it so I went in through the little window that I always go through and saw my brother, Pepper. He asked me where I had been all this time and I told him. Pepper said our pets must have gone far, far away on holiday and would be coming back in a few sleeps time. I settled down to sleep. We waited and waited and slept and slept until eventually they all came back, and then I hugged and kissed them and I never wanted them to go away for the day again!

School of the Dead

by Sonny Wilson

Have you ever felt really cold? I don't mean like a winter type cold, I'm talking about a very rare cold. A cold that makes you feel frozen, so you can't think, you can't talk, but most of all you can't run. If you've had this feeling, I suggest you put this book down straight away and cry for help, tell someone, anyone, otherwise they will get you! You may have picked this up at a local book shop or been lent it by a family friend and you are probably thinking this is a book of fiction, but they only put that on the cover so people would read it back, but no, this is a book of truth.

My name is Ryan and I'm fifteen years old. I go to St Mary's school. I have only one friend, called Max. We met when we were eight and she's been my only friend ever since. At school we can't be separated. We do everything together.

It was a bright sunny morning and I had just walked into the school when I noticed something a little odd. I saw a small boy dressed all in black trying to open my locker. He looked way too young to be at the school. The second I looked at him my body froze as he started to slowly turn his head: then I saw it: he had no face, just a shadow. When he turned towards me, I tried desperately to look away, but I was frozen. My head was pounding, I was terrified. Then, suddenly he was gone. I almost collapsed and gasped for air. One of the girls looked at me as if I was an idiot. I ran to the toilet and splashed my face with water. How could I explain what I'd seen?

Later, I came out of my lesson to go to lunch when I saw Max. I grabbed her by the hand and pulled her into a doorway of the maths classroom.

"I've got something to tell you," we both said to each other in unison. I told her what had happened and she said she'd had exactly the same experience, but she'd seen a strange girl, not a boy, near her locker, just outside the girls toilets. At that moment Mr Wilson came over to us and said in a firm voice we had to get to lunch.

Although I often think of it, we never spoke of what we saw ever again.

A Book

by Henry Atkinson

I possessed a name previously but now it appears I may as well be
number nine. I remember the whole interaction with somewhat
grim detail, as though it all happened yesterday, clichéd though that
may sound. It started as a pleasant yet windy day and I had decided
to drive out and take a walk in the forest. Paying close attention to
the design of the woods I looked upon the ecosystem with a faulty
smile: the small grey squirrels jumping from branch to branch, the
faint flutter of birds' wings and the effervescence spirit of the distant
deer, frolicking with one another. Looking upwards, I couldn't help
but notice the deep grey skies to my left and conscious of the
direction in which the strong wind was headed I took a turn home. It
can't have been more than fifty feet after this turn that I spotted a
clearing with a most tranquil looking pond; calling for me to briefly
inspect the treasure nature had left for me. The pond was about eight
feet wide and almost appeared to be artificial upon further inspection.

A beautiful formation of rocks and boulders shielded the pocket
of heaven which was surrounded by trees, grass and thriving wildlife.
The tree too was at this paradise; a colossal affair by any standard
and one of the many reasons why nature's enormity should be feared.
Drawing closer to the pond no more than a few yards away from it I

spotted an unnaturally large book. A leather case with what looked like a small fat lion on the front, some unknown exciting creature. I opened this book only to be stunned at the sacred writing as any would be or have been. Flicking through each individual page despite not having a clue what on earth I was looking at. Tracing with my finger each character I recognised as new to me. Tempted as I was to simply dip a toe in the decadence of the pond, I refrained from doing so, though a similar fate may have been met nevertheless. With my excitement I instead insisted on looking for the origins of this book. I naturally assumed that as the book was dry it was not from the pond and with the only other notable landmark in sight being the grotesque, obnoxious, oversized, eyesore of this tree. I looked here. I walked hesitantly toward and at about three feet away the tree slowly became translucent until it was no more. I froze, and then I ran. I ran, leaving the car I had driven here in my panic, about twelve miles home. I ran twelve miles in shattering rain, soaking wet, panting like a frightened beast. Upon finally reaching my destination I fumbled the key until it fit the lock and collapsed in my landing slamming the door behind me, stunned in disbelief. Despite the excess of intoxication I still remember every second of panic from that night. Two days passed in this state of dismay and fear.

Three mornings afterwards, having remembered my car, I ordered a taxi to help me collect it and sadly my car had gone and in its place instead was this damned book. I grabbed the book in anger and threw it to the floor into the dirt and mud, secretly coveting what the pages meant. I rode back in complete silence clenching my fists, willing to fight the tree. I'm certain that at some point or another my driver asked several questions but I said nothing and instead looked out of the window. As we drove away I spotted this tree that towered the forest and without a moment's hesitation I began to cry.

Upon reflection these tears may seem ridiculous but I am sure you can share my struggle. Seeing an object, harmless and innocent though it may be, disappear does have an effect on the mental state. I cried for what must have been hours begging to the sky to tell me what I had seen and what it meant and what I might do but as always there was no answer. I slumped outside of my humble cottage in the garden with the fresh green grass and in the dead of night I began to cut the grass with a large mower I store in my stained wood shed. If you were to ask me why I did this I could still not give an answer but something compelled me to do so. Some higher power perhaps possessed me or perhaps I had just gone mad. And the next day I saw it. I saw this tree. This colossal tree towering over my garden with an angelic pond and a dull leather book. I left the house of course without flinching. I considered burning the whole thing down but realised the bother I might have gotten myself in doing so. I wish I had burned everything. I felt depressed wandering the streets and seeing behind every tower block a massive tree; larger than the sky scrapers when I looked up. It almost seemed to grow in enormity as I tried to escape it. I became a beggar for several weeks ignoring my day job until I was presumed dead (I never heard from them again) and with no close family I was unnoticed. Soon the boredom of a beggar set in and I finally caved, accepting the tree that followed me everywhere. In shame I walked home and confronted the tree. I walked towards it, my heart pounding out of my chest and after a prolonged hesitation, I touch it. It remains physical for a second before again changing and dragging me through it.

The next moments are forgotten by me but I woke up what felt like years later in total darkness and remained motionless until I could hear the blood flowing around my body at speed. The encompassing darkness was so black that I was confused as to whether or not my eyes were open or shut. The watch I had before was now completely shattered and no longer functioned at keeping the time. The only purpose it served was to give me something to look at as the slowly fading 'glow in the dark' hands of the watch spun with the earth's gravity until finally the light that had been stored as energy had dissipated and darkness remained. I finally reached clumsily around myself before I finally found a stick that I guessed was maybe a few feet in length. I eventually decided that wherever I was could be bested and so I used the stick to guide myself around the absence of light only to find that I could move freely and seemingly infinitely around the area. Yet, the cavern was not empty for I saw a beatific aspect in the distance in the form of a radiant blue mushroom that reached four foot off the ground. In want of sustenance, I took a bite of the bland fungus and it turned my stomach despite my starvation. From this mushroom I saw hundreds more following a trail. Varying colours and shapes of lit up fungi each one between three and eight foot assisted in my navigation as though a mythical forest surrounded me. I finally was met with an orange glow of fire, though the flame was small and nought but embers with a fire pit that had a circumference of no more than a few inches. I used the tasteless mushrooms to grow the fire into a peaceful place where I could sit and regain my warmth before venturing further through this magical ecosystem.

The next leg of my expedition was with a torch made of the mushrooms which burnt profitably. I marked various small holes in the walls that seemed to rustle with my own movement. They were plotting. I aimlessly walked further before hearing a distant rumble. Despite my instinct of fear I followed the rumble and appeared at a river. The running water seemed so angelic and sublime I stopped to observe the bright blue liquid that ran gaily and for a moment I began to feel unwatched. I used the water to quench my thirst. Though food was still an issue in this barren system aside from the rubber, light-emitting mushrooms that encompassed me. It was at this point I felt at my most solitary when suddenly four fat impish creatures, ten inches tall and disproportionately wide, appeared as enigmas in the corner of my eye. I listened to hear the tongue they spoke to each other in, but their tone was reminiscent of conniving. I could not respond to their words even if I understood what cryptic language they spoke, for I was so struck with awe at the creatures I froze and gazed emptily into their black eyes. They ran with haste despite their small unfit stature and disappeared into the mushroom fields surrounding me. I sat alone with my dying torch before finally recollecting the strength to push through the seemingly tranquil current of the river. As I waded through the water, I heard a deep grumble from the unpleased earth and a current of overwhelming strength swept me from my feet downstream in a dazed flurry. Survival became a priority and I felt the adrenaline surge through me. All my feelings of wonder had neglected the outlandish nature of the foreign land I was in and suddenly, I played the fool. Being carried by the river in darkness and drowning slowly I met a sheer drop where the stream transformed to a waterfall sending me to a sure demise.

Sadly, it was not there that I died but it shall be instead where I woke after this sheer drop. I remember fading in and out of consciousness being moved with logs on a wooden platform surrounded by theses disgusting trolldren. The same fat grotesque creatures I met down by the riverside only, I remember, I witnessed a sight of pure beauty before I fell asleep and awoke here. A tree with thousands of glowing lanterns on the end of each branch with an elegant female figure garnished in green slumped gracefully atop the tree of life. She looked into my eyes giving me a feeling of utmost euphoria before I was swept away.

Now I'm here. I was merely teased with the vision of a utopia. I awoke on a harsh rock floor with a measly heap of foul hay and in the far corner of the room eight perfectly preserved bodies. The bodies had no distinct odour and each corpse is still wearing the clothes they entered this infernal tree with. I roused myself in good spirits having the glorious sight previously, but my elation was met with depression and a mound of former living beings now as cold and still as the rock they lie on. I marvelled at the sight of a burning candle that's flame has thus far been everlasting. The superhuman nature of my entire setting became apparent to me with this mere flame. Upon following the flame, I met this book. The same: rough, brown, leather book only this time it was encircled by blue dust which caused the book to emit an abnormal blue flame that is without heat. I opened the book to gaze once more upon the enchanted writing. Yet, as I turned each page the letters deciphered forming varying hand writing with each from varying time periods. Charles from Victorian England who states he is in charge of a mine where children work for pennies. Walter, a lumberjack with a wife and two daughters. An urge to document my experience met me upon looking at the book, and so I grabbed the quill, dipped in red ink beside me, and began writing. I have no water to survive with, so I am destined to perish soon, no doubt. Spin your tale as I have spun mine, meaningless though it may be. At least it can entertain ones ultimate moments as the stories before me have. Consoling in the misfortune of the fellow innocents that have suffered a similar if not worse fate than thee.

Silas Venus-Haslett

Cheoticus

by Silas Venus-Haslett

Compared to disastrous natural events and beasts twice our size, humanity as a whole is nothing but bacteria compared to the gargantuan size of the Universe. Who knows what kinds of fantastic entities lie beyond the stars and across the multiverse: entities with god-like powers and intellect beyond our comprehension.

What I saw that one fateful night will haunt me for the rest of my existence. It was January 3rd, 1989 and I was making my way down to an inn at the end of the town during my stay on the west coast of Ireland. The White Wagon was the name of the inn and as I was strolling towards it I saw a man crouching with his head in his hands repeating the same thing over and over.

"The bandage man, the bandage man!"

I clearly thought he was delirious or at least had too much to drink as he had a great many beer bottles lying beside him.

I continued into The White Wagon, casually making my way to the bar for a well-earned drink. I sat down next to a man who looked somewhat in shock as if he had just witnessed something terrible. He was old, had a snow-white beard and by the look of his cap, was perhaps a sailor. Minding my own business I ignored him and asked the barman for a drink. To my surprise the man turned and stared at me.

"Hey, do you believe in the supernatural?" he said.

I was confused, but curious as to why he asked me, a complete stranger, such an odd question.

"No, but why do you ask?" I questioned, wanting to hear more. He looked around to see if anyone was listening.

"I have seen something. Something along the coast, striding along the sand," he said. "It was like a man, but taller, must have been over nine feet tall and its body was hidden under layers of bandages."

At this point I remembered the drunk outside and the way he had repeated 'the bandage man.'

"Layers of bandages did you say?" I asked, fascinated by this peculiar description.

"Oh yes. It was wearing a black, ripped up cloak and its hands and face were completely covered in bandages except for this one weird eye," the old sailor continued, "And now that was the strangest part: its one eye was glowing as if it were on fire. The other eye being covered."

Noticing my incredulity at this tale, he leant in towards me, on the verge of anger.

"I know what I saw mister, and whatever it was that crossed the sand, I am certain…" the old man paused to take a drink. "…it was no man."

This intrigued me somewhat. I finished my beer and left the inn. As I strolled down the street towards the beach, I saw a very unsettling symbol freshly daubed on the side of a building. It was bright red and in the shape of an eye, not a human eye as the pupil was a slit instead of round. The pupil was peculiarly surrounded by what could have been a ring of flame but on looking closer I became worried as to what it was made from. The markings were still wet and as I ran my finger against it, I knew exactly what the sticky substance was… blood.

What could this burning eye mean and why was it drawn in blood, and more importantly, what or whose blood had been used? I looked around me and started to pick up my pace, thinking about this strange, bandaged figure with the glowing eye and the blood-stained symbol I'd just seen. I became more anxious, but curious, with a disturbing feeling like I was being watched. Perhaps that was what the symbol represented. Could it have been what traumatised the fishermen? As I made my way past the dimming street lights into the docks I noticed that they were completely abandoned: the empty boats were rocking back and forth in the water, the shops and houses lifeless, lightless and locked shut.

I made my way towards the cliff top and the steps that led down to the sandy beaches with a hope to perhaps uncover more about this curious mystery and strange entity that had reportedly been sighted. As I stumbled down the damp rocky steps, covered in seaweed and barnacles, I saw more blood-stained drawings of the same burning eye symbol on the sea wall. Once on the seashore, I followed the symbols along the overhanging cliff to find it open into a large dark cavern. Looking within I laid my unprepared eyes onto a shocking sight which I will, unfortunately, never forget: in the pool that filled this cave were dozens of mangled dead bodies.

The foul stench of these rotting corpses along with the strong salt from the water almost made me vomit. I was traumatised and had to keep myself from mentally breaking, but I had a drive to figure out what was really going on. As I stumbled backwards out of the cave in a state of shock, I made my way at first aimlessly along the sandy beach. Then I glimpsed a fire just around the headland glowing behind the salty rocks of the next bay, encouraging me to investigate.

When I got around the rocks I moved closer towards a large boulder where I spotted writing on its surface, once again, painted in blood from some poor victim whose body was probably disposed of in the cavern with the other lost souls. As I read the text, chills went up my spine.

"All wrapped up in bandages and black robes, the beast now and then comes and goes, rarely revealing his inhuman face he searches for human souls to taste, from across the stars scouring the cosmos he torments minds and brings chaos, with great intellect and god-like abilities he has no fear or vulnerabilities, his name is Cheoticus."

I was befuddled as to what I had just read to myself. Cheoticus? What was this so called god-like creature? What did it mean to come from beyond our galaxy and if true, what could such a being possibly want? In the dark I felt it to be real and was terrified by the thought of an alien entity so far beyond our normal comprehension.

As I leaned my head slowly around the rock to look upon the fire, I witnessed people dressed in purple robes with hoods obscuring their faces. The centre of their chests on their unsettling cloaks were emblazoned with the same symbol of the eye with the burning pupil in gold fabric. They were chanting, screaming, raising their arms in the air in some sort of demonic cult ceremony. Then without any warning the fire went out and it was pitch black. I stood in trepidation, waiting to see what obscure turn of events could possibly happen next. Then I saw tiny sparks of electricity appear where the fire had been, growing larger and more rapid, the energy started forming into the shape of a sphere, but in a rapid flash and a blinding light the electrical ball quickly expanded and opened into some sort of demonic portal.

I was in awe. It was unlike anything I'd ever gazed upon in my life. The rotating doorway made of powerful energy gave off a strangely beautiful bright lime green light onto the rocks and sand. All the worshippers fell to their knees, their heads bowed low and the portal began to flicker like a lightbulb that was just about to go out. It was at this point when He stepped out onto the damp sand and stood tall but silent with His one glowing eye, as if it were on fire, focusing on the men and women worshipping before him. He must have stood over nine feet tall. His hands and face were all wrapped up except that one blazing eye. He wore a ripped black cloak, hiding the shape of His body. Cheoticus had entered our world.

Something hung around his neck: a medallion of gold with that hateful flaming-eyed symbol etched into the metal. That's what it all meant. I could see it now. The bloody markings were representing the entity Himself. The hideous thing pointed at one of the cultists and indicated that she come closer. What happened next, as she stepped towards the dreadful Cheoticus, towering over her as if she was a child, will haunt me for the rest of my life. His flaming eye began to widen and bandages covering his face began to unravel, slowly piling onto the sand revealing a nightmarish face that would turn the strongest of stomachs. There was revealed a dozen or more multiple eyes, shining bright like fireballs spread out across an oozing tar-black face, with snake-like tendrils flailing out of the head. I couldn't move, I was petrified, frozen in terror by the unholy sight of Cheoticus. The disgusting black tentacles latched on to the women's face, sticking to her like thick black spider silk. The woman's screams were short-lived, muffled as more and more tendrils wrapped around her face like a cocoon. Then, as the vile, flickering tentacles removed themselves from the women's head all that was left was a dry hollow skull. There was no skin, no eyes, no muscles, not even a drop of blood was remaining on her domed white head. I felt so sick and retched in disgust, loud enough for both the remaining cultists and Cheoticus to hear me. The beast turned at once to face me with His multiple eyes, the tentacles on his face jolted and squirmed in a sense of rage and I was stunned. Then a deep, shuddering voice echoed inside my mind.

"I see you."

The creature could somehow communicate with me directly into my mind. I broke free of His gaze and turned to sprint as fast as I could across the beach, splashing through the incoming tide, into the pitch black night. I did not look back even when I managed to make it to the solitary room of my own lodgings. I trembled in fear from the tip of my head to the bottom of my toes for some time before climbing to bed exhausted. I drifted into a dreamless sleep.

Not a day goes by when I don't think of that awful night: the bodies in the pool, witnessing the death and that eldritch abomination's inhuman face. I returned to the beach a few days later in broad daylight. I could not find the cavern, the rocks or any part of the coast that resembled where I had been that night. Did I, like the sailors, have too much to drink that night? Did I ingest some malignant poison? I think not. I fear instead that I am losing my mind to Cheoticus as when the lights go out and the night is quiet, I still see that burning eye and still hear that terrible voice.

"I can see you."

Now I have returned to the City and live among its bright lights and loud noises; they keep the fear at bay for the most part. But when it gets dark and when it gets quiet, all I can think about is how long I have left to live before He calls me again.

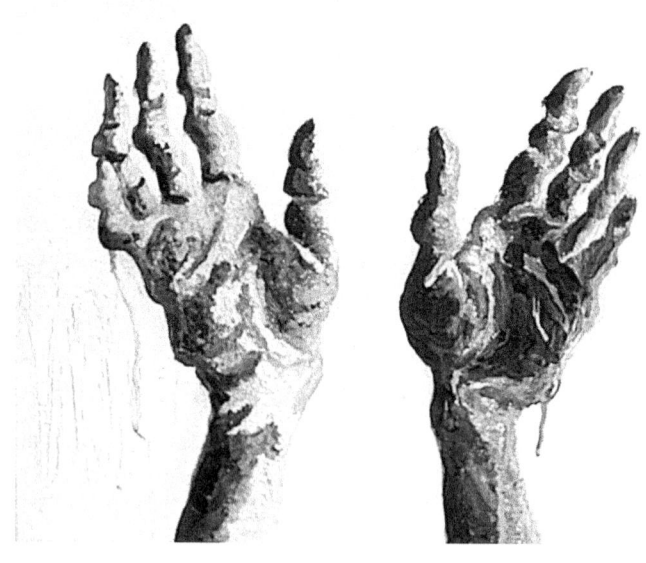

Paula Hattenkerl

Autumn's Cold

by Annabel Head

The splintered wood of the bench ran under my blue fingertips as the final traces of summer lingered in the air. Autumn with its vibrant leaves and cooling had taken its toll over everything: bending and shaping green leaves into crispy, crunchy, colourful ones, filling shop shelves with harvest produce and casting the smell of cinnamon in the atmosphere.

The cold spat and hit at my pink tinted cheeks. As I wandered around the place my memories came to life. I remember running around on the grass and jumping into a sea of orange. Autumn was always my favourite season. I remember the sights and smells and sounds of the park; my park. My special park that I used to visit everyday with her.

She used to wrap me up in layers of colourful wool that was made for only me. She used to make me hot chocolate after prancing around in the autumn weather with me. She would smile as she saw me after a long day. Her smile was better than any words in any language.

Even though I loved autumn, the cold didn't love me. I dug my chapped hands into my coat pocket, hugging it for some sort of warmth. My fingers sunk into a soft material: gloves. I pulled out the bundle of knitted wool and examined the blue, aged items as I felt a smile stretch onto my face. Time had abused them but the pure sight of the gloves grabbed the oldest memories from my mind.

The cold continued to bite at any part of flesh that wasn't covered by my clothes, but I stopped caring. She would always say that this weather was just any excuse to make hot chocolate. I laughed at the thought of her goofy nature. How could I have forgotten her? I almost forgot about her existence while I was away. It started with letters from her every day, but as time left behind small details in history, her letters became less frequent. One a day, one a month, one a year, never another one.

I heard a squeak of a swing and I was suddenly grabbed back into my childhood. The sound of the swings that I adored. She would push me on them, insisted that I needed her. I remember the one time I retaliated. I clutched my cheek as the stinging sensation returned. My brain suddenly recalled the way she would spit and shout at me for no reason. Or was it that I wasn't doing anything?

After that one sour thought, I was reminded of another bad memory, then that one thought turned into twenty, then one hundred, until my head started spinning and my heart rate sped up. I snapped. My eyes were no longer blinded by my past.

I stood in the middle of a destroyed wasteland. The trees that used to be full of colour were now withered and the autumn grass was stained with the debris of an explosion. It had been five years since I was sent to war. Everything was gone. The once smooth surface was now littered with craters. They had taken away everything; the only thing I had left was my inaccurate imagination.

The hateful cold stopped attacking me and seemed almost to comfort me as I circled back to the bench. It seemed different, out of place even. I couldn't remember it. Why had my mind omitted this single bench? I read the writing on the cheap metal plaque and I stopped in shock. Reaching out, I touched it to confirm it was reality. The splintered wood of the bench ran under my blue fingertips as the final traces of war lingered in the air. Time itself seemed to stop as I stood in front of the memorial for my mother.

Silas Venus-Haslett

The Gatekeeper

by Manfred Kong

I t was a beautiful sunset, followed by the evening breeze. The Moon glowing, slightly covered by the clouds. Wind was howling through the trees.

The big house in the forest needed a gatekeeper. Emmanuel needed a job, so he went up to the old mansion, a massive house, with a huge garden. There had been a story about a killer in the forest. Emmanuel thought that it was probably this reason that the house needed a guard. He knocked on the old wooden door and five minutes later a beautiful young lady opened it. They didn't have much of a conversation, just enough for him to get the job.

The next day, he went back. He sat in the little guard shed next to the big old rusty gate. The silence hit him straight away. He was to simply sit there, staring into the endless forest, night after night. It was boring work, but it was very good pay so he kept on going back, night after night. Just sitting there staring into the darkness. Nothing ever changed except for the sound of some animals moving somewhere out there in the forest. It was too dark to see them.

One night, he went to work as usual. He sat down in his guard chair and started staring out once more. Just after midnight a point of light appeared in the end of the forest. It was faint but just about noticeable, occasionally flashing. Emmanuel wondered what it could be, but he did not leave his post. The next night, the same thing happened. This time the light was brighter, closer. Emmanuel became more alert. It was still so silent.

Night after night, the light seemed closer and closer, brighter and brighter. One night it was raining heavily. The light was now close enough to see it was a torch. It was being held by the young lady who had given him the job. She wasn't moving; she just stood there in the middle of the woods, staring at him. Emmanuel was confused. He stood up and left the guard shed, the heavy rain drenching him, cold and wet. He walked towards the young lady, calling out, hoping for a response, an explanation. Emmanuel stood face to face with her. She did not speak. She just stared directly into his eyes. She gave out a sudden piercing scream. Then he noticed that she was carrying a long knife in her other hand. She plunged it into his heart. Emmanuel fell to the ground. The woman dragged the body back to the mansion, leaving a trail of blood up to the house which was soon washed away by the rain. The woman closed the old wooden door behind her and silence fell in the forest.

It was a beautiful sunset, followed by the evening breeze. The Moon glowing, slightly covered by the clouds. Wind was howling through the trees. The big house in the slaughtering forest needed another guard, another gatekeeper.

Martin and the Well

by Ruby Wormwold

Martin stared up looking at the huge wall of bricks towering over him. Behind lay a long stretch of land belonging to The Orchards (that was the name of the house) which included a dark and queer forest, as far as the eye could see. Then a thrust of wind came from the West, sending a chill down his spine. He was not sure (and that was for certain) about moving into the house, but his parents really wanted to buy it. Back in Barroness (which was the town that he used to live in) all of his friends had told him rumours about... Oh it's too frightening to tell.

His Mum and Dad were busy unpacking when Martin called out, "Mum, I'm going to have a look around the garden." As soon as those words had left his mouth he regretted them. He realised that his mother would probably find him something useful to do, so he darted off in the direction of the forest.

At the edge of the wood, he stared at the dark muddy path leading far into the distance and deep and deep into the wood itself.

Martin stepped into the forest daringly, the sticky mud squelching every dreaded step he took.

Before he had gone far, suddenly Martin heard a very faint noise in the distance as if a penny had dropped on the uneven ground. He stopped in silence for a while, until he was adamant that his mind was playing tricks on him. Still, he was hesitant about moving forward, but decided to continue. The rumours had surely been wrong. He was quite far into the woodland by now when he came to a sudden change of direction in the walkway, as it turned immediately to the left. Only five more minutes he walked, trying to prove that there was nothing to be scared of when he heard a voice screaming in the distance, distraught and put a stop in his tracks. Now he really wanted to turn back. He decided to lick his finger and put it up to the wind. The wind was flowing like a sea of water gushing the way he was facing. So he turned around and kept walking in the direction of the wind determined to find his house again. He went on for a while, trying to block out the screaming. Martin started to run faster.

An old-fashioned well came into view. He eventually slowed, stumbling as he went. He then stopped. The scream seemed to be coming from the well. The darkness fell around Martin like a slow tornado sweeping through his hair and clothes. Then the scream came to a complete halt, as if the scream knew he was there. Martin looked around and caught a glimpse of a shiny object through the corner of his eye. At the top of a large, old and dead oak tree (almost falling over because of how much it was leaning to the left) there seemed to be a bracelet or necklace, something glinting and catching the light. Martin wanted to find out what the item was but he didn't want to climb the tree because it was so precious. So he clutched a rock in his hand and threw it at the branch, that was holding the item like a hand in the air. The branch came crashing down plunging to the ground. He quickly snatched it up and found it to be a penny. He then found another four pennies on the ground. Each penny was handmade of gold metal that had writing on it. The first penny read "BE CAREFUL" the second read "WHAT" and if you put all the words together from each penny, it read, "BE CAREFUL WHAT YOU WISH FOR." Martin was curious, but strangely excited.

Quickly he flicked a penny in the well and said to himself, "I wish for infinite money." Just then, in the blink of an eye a voice shouted out, "I never got what I wanted, so why should you?"

Then millions and millions of pound notes from many years ago came flying out of the well... and every single note was cut up into tiny pieces. Martin was disappointed so he tried and tried again. Each time the object he wished for came out in pieces.

Before long he only had two pennies left and threw one in the well. This time he was smart. He did not wish for a physical object, but decided for him and his family to live forever.

Fourteen years later, a couple came to look around The Orchards. They were in a hurry so one said, "I'll have a look round the house and you go and a have a look around the garden."

Each set off eagerly. The lady who was looking round the garden found the well. She peered in, but now deep in the well, all she could see was a large pile of what looked like bones and a glimpse of what seemed to be a coin. A gust of wind sent a shiver down her spine. She then heard a noise, it seemed to be someone whispering, quietly murmuring, "Be careful what you wish for."

The People
of Mars

by Konrad Lüdecke

2030 – Mars. Unpopulated, orange, completely pale. There appeared a white dot on the sky. It came closer and closer, reaching the planet very slowly. As it gets to Mars, you can see it more clearly: it is a spaceship. It was sent six weeks ago. It lands with an enormous dust cloud, but the spacecraft itself is not too big, maybe the size of a small house. A few minutes later the door opens. An astronaut is stepping out onto the surface area of Mars for the very first time. This moment gets broadcasted all over the world, the leftover world, with the world cities called Cairo, Nairobi and Pretoria.

A few years before it all started, the Earth had been completely wasted. There had been a nuclear war in Europe. The middle east was run by a terroristic state. The American economy collapsed and south east Asia suffered from a devastating virus. Only Africa had survived without a big crisis. This was a new experience for all people living there. Suddenly they had the most resources, money and power, as the rest of the world was in big trouble. There was a new revolutionary action throughout Africa, because for the first time in history all governments of the African nations worked together, as one big, peaceful party. The people there felt happy and free for perhaps the first time. They didn't have to think about where they were getting their next meal from or how to earn money. It was all there. So they used their minds to think about how to carry on with the world. They thought about the rise in population, which made Africa too small for all the people wanting to live there and assessed multiple ways to expand their land. As there was crisis in all other parts of their once so beloved Earth, they had to check other alternatives. The one closest by was, to populate Mars.

Financed by their collective resources, the smartest people of the continent managed to create a working spaceship by 2022. Two years previously, in 2020, they managed to construct the world's first efficient nuclear fusion reactor, small enough to fit in a spaceship. Since then, for the next years they trained the astronauts and readied on the spaceship.

Then 2030 finally arrived, and the first men and women ever in history, all Africans, touched down on Mars.

The Good Place

by Fran Sutterby

I screamed. I yelled. I thrashed. Not even a coarse whisper escaped my lips. No one was near me when I awoke. No one but a weasel-like brown haired man in a tired suit who clutched a stethoscope making him seem important. I reached out to grab his hand as he stormed past my bed, but my arm did not move. Nor did my leg. My head was glued to the pillow and I was not even sure I had any feet attached to my long skinny legs anymore. My eyes became heavy once again. I could feel myself drifting into a drug-induced slumber.

It was a pleasant summer's day and the sun was starting to set, creating an array of colours on the bland baby blue background. The sky had melded into the ocean as they joined hands on the horizon, but was now starting to differ as the colours of the sunset split across the sky. Long tanned grass brushed past my knees. The wind tickled my body from head to toe as it made the leaves from the towering trees spiral to the floor with only a gently whisper. I could hear them whistle past my ear in a calm frenzy of fun. It was Autumn that I could taste. Autumn in its full colours.

The leaves crunched under my step as I sauntered, creating the sound that all toddlers cherish, bringing me further into the depth of my memories. I was six again and the warming aroma of coffee that lingered in the room was the only thing I could taste. The rich dark and roasted smell floated around the dim room and the trickle of the tap and the buzz of the fridge and the crackling spit of the fire all echoed around the four walls of the room, enveloping me in a blanket of fond memories.

The buzz of lights, the murmur of voices and the overwhelming smell of disinfectant was all I noticed when I came to. I was dazed and disoriented. Lost and bewildered. My strength had drained from me in those endless few minutes that had drifted by. I had achieved nothing but at least in my mind I was awake.

A bird jumped into flight, presumably to deliver its latest meal to its kin. Pigments of black were splattered across its back which shimmered a metallic blue when the sun bounced off it, just like a magpie. I had dreamed of being in the sky, flying with the birds and bouncing on the clouds as I gazed longingly up at the pretty bird that flew above me.

BANG. A bullet ricocheted around my brain, shattering the comforting darkness that rested in my mind, destroying the child-like happiness that was now so alien to me. My memory replayed its loop: the shouts, the shots, the screams. Every single day since I woke up. Again and again.

People crowded me but did not try to look at me: for what they saw was not me. Hidden, somewhere under those many layers of confusion, was a little girl who had a warm bed at home and two pairs of furry slippers tucked neatly next to it.

I saw them reach for the switch, as I pointlessly screamed in a silent hysteria. I saw my life flicker like a candle, volatile and erratic. I felt the machine skip a beat, followed by another, and another, until there were no more. The little girl with the slippers who once had entered this room was no more.

Numbness covered me and darkness engulfed my body. You'd think I'd be glad to leave the pain behind: but at least pain meant you knew it was real. I much preferred the other place. The place that I visited only in my mind. The good place.

But maybe now I could fly with the birds. High up in the sky. That's where they were. Maybe now I wouldn't have to dream.

Silas Venus-Haslett

Downtown 61

by Archie Robinson

For a moment there was nothing. He just had to wait. Then, it hit. It was a Tsar hydrogen bomb; the most powerful bomb in the world, and it had just split the sky in half.

Taz was 80 miles out of the city, which was far enough away not to die. For a few seconds there was just a blinding light a few hundred miles off. Then the light began to grow and grow. Soon there was a dreadful rumble and the ground around him began to shake, as if the ground was a drum and it had just been hit. Then the shockwave came. You could almost see it as a haze in the distance hurtling towards you at hundreds of miles per hour. It smashed into Taz like a bull, lifting him up like a doll and dropping him back into the ground.

When he could get up he saw that the whole of the southern horizon was on fire. All of it. A huge pillar of fire, higher than Everest, in the middle. Taz just lay on the ground, in awe of the sheer destruction around him, helpless, and cried while all around more explosions were going off around him.

He had lain there for what seemed like hours, but could have been just minutes until, eventually, he picked himself up and started walking. London was still burning and the air was full of ash and smoke which made him cough and splutter. He wasn't quite sure what he should do so he picked a direction and walked.

He had no food or water and was terrified; there were still distant booms going on all around. After walking for a time (he didn't know how long) he saw some activity on the top of a hill. As he approached he saw people moving about there and lots of cars driving away. Becoming hopeful and realising that he might not die, he sped up and once he was close enough, a man saw him and started to jog towards him.

"You all right?" the man said.

Taz nodded slowly.

"You'd better come into the base," said the man. He started to walk in the direction of the town. "Are you coming or what?"

There were lots of people in the town. Most of them looked dazed and empty. He realised that he probably looked the same. He was taken into a big building which had probably been a storage warehouse before, but had been converted to temporary accommodation. There were lots of mats on the floor which must serve as beds and tables in the corner with people eating a sort of slop sitting around them, talking quietly. The man took him to a table which wasn't full and sat him down, then went over to a big barrel with a bowl and came back with a bowl of the slop which everybody else seemed to be eating. The people at the table stared at him and then one asked, "Where did you come from?"

"London," he replied, staring down into his bowl.

They exchanged murmurs and quick glances.

"Nobody else came back from London."

He had a rough night full of nightmares about the explosions. When he woke, he thought he was still in London and when he remembered he felt as if he had been punched. All of the emotion which he had not felt was washing over him in torrents and he had to lie down again to stop himself from fainting. Eventually, he got up and walked over to the table he had been sleeping next to and got himself a bowl of slop. Once he had eaten, several men came into the warehouse and called out the names of some people. He was among them. They looked around expectantly and the people whose names had been called out began to stand up.

"Pack your things. You're being moved out."

Taz saw the others packing their things and suddenly felt sad. He himself had nothing. After everyone else had finished packing, the men led them out and onto the dirt road outside the building and onto a convoy of trucks. Taz was loaded onto the first truck in the line and took a seat. There was a large man sitting at the front driving the vehicle and he looked around at Taz. "We're taking you off to Downtown 61, one of the new places. You're that London kid, aren't you?"

"Yes," he replied.

The man turned around and murmured, "No one else came back from London."

A few hours later, after drifting off to sleep, Taz was suddenly awoken by a loud crack. He bolted upright and saw the driver slumped forward in his seat, blood leaking from his chest. Then he heard a bang behind him. There was shouting outside, and his truck was veering off into the side of the road. The truck slammed into a bank and came to a stop. Moments later, the back doors flung open and people started shooting inside. Taz saw several of the people who he had been sitting next to on the floor, dead and several others screaming. He opened the side door and jumped out. It was pure carnage. Two of the trucks in the convoy were on fire and another was torn in half. There were people running everywhere and bullets whipping through the air. Taz ran to the bank his truck had crashed into and jumped over it. He didn't know what to do, so he just started running. Running as fast as he could.

Taz ran and ran for miles, until he came to a sign: 'Downtown 61 - 20 miles.' His hopes had just started to rise slightly, with the chance of peace at last, when he heard a deafening roar. He looked up and saw a pillar of fire towering up into the sky, splitting it in half and then a wall of fire. A wall speeding towards him at hundreds of miles an hour. He had lost everything. It wouldn't matter if he lost just one more thing. He closed his eyes and simply embraced it.

Bananas

by Asa Jones

"Bananas," he thought to himself, the concept sounded familiar. "Bananas, I've forgotten the bananas!" This sudden revelation was replaced in his head as fast as the keys in his hand fell onto his bare feet. After realising something even more important, he dashed, finger first, toward the 'On' button of his desktop computer. His left index finger compresses against the circular indent. The monster is released, roaring into action. "Dave was right," he thought as he grasped the sides of his dark brown leather chair. "Banana is exactly what I need."

Banana, for those not attuned to the latest electrical jargon, is described by the Magazine 'Hashtags, At symbols and that weird thing above the backwards slash' as the single neatest, well written, most pointless piece of coding ever developed; it simply does nothing. But our hero had never heard of 'Hashtag, At symbols and that weird thing above the backwards slash.' No, he learnt of Banana from Dave (see above) at work. Dave then heard about it from Shirley at the NHS Sheffield Minor emergencies call centre, who in turn heard it mentioned on the BBC's hit new show "Yo Moma," and other weird things we said as children.'" which eventually took its information from Shadow (Note: English Literature students should notice that the scene of foreboding created from the name, 'Shadow' is emphasised by the contrast with the comedic tone set by the rest of the paragraph. (Sub-note: Just in case you're not paying attention , we will see the Shadow later. (Sub-sub-note: sorry, spoilers))). Ultimately, this means that our hero is now in the understanding that 'banana' will make his computer able to emulate Apple software. Something very useful to the hero as his company made the very stupid mistake several years ago of switching over to Macs.

Nevertheless, he sat there (as he did almost every day) watching the faint, white text – disclaiming the computer's load up protocol – flash before his eyes. Then they would stop. The words 'Setting up Desktop' sprayed across the screen. He always liked these words, disregarding the fact that their being there so long meant his computer was older than his daughter (a fact he often felt ashamed of). No, these words were safe. They remained there with him, comrades in arms waiting to go 'over the top.' Then, the monster by his feet began to crescendo with a final clearing of the throat, allowing the screen to fill with icons and taskbars. He glided his mouse over to the start button. The menu bursts from the bottom of the screen, at the top the letters 'Jeffery Frederickson' are displayed in bold, assertive letters signifying a small sense of self pride within himself. He drives his mouse over to Internet Explorer, lets out a short chuckle and flies back to Google Chrome.

Despite Jeffery's great pride in his computer, he always reasoned that the low value of the device implied that it simply deserved no protection. On the contrary, it is often the weakest computers that are the most vulnerable. However, as becomes customary with Jeffery, he simply decided to disregard the truth (Fun Factoid: The Café where Jeffery's wife meets with her friends to protest Jeffery's constant incompetence uses the X-543a model of coffee machine where as the rest of the franchise uses the X-544c. Thus this gives the coffee a sweeter taste, often making the disputing women slightly sadistic within their debates. (Sub-Factoid: Jeffery takes his coffee with two sugars.)) Back to the point, this means every time Jeffery loads Chrome, he is used to ads, 'messages,' spam (not the Viking kind) and security messages appearing. However, today was different.

As Jeffery carelessly closed off the endless sea of spam, spam, spam, spam… he was surprised to see a different window appear in the centre of his screen. Initially, he assumed another virus had wriggled its way into the circuitry. Even the official style of the pop-up didn't faze him; he simply thought ads were getting smarter. But just as he leaned his mouse towards the cross in the corner, he noticed the text in the middle of the window and froze. Slowly, the warm optimism the concept of 'Banana' brought was overrun by the wintry, stale letters before him: "Jeffery, help!"

Carolina Clements

Grace's Doll

by Phoebe Russell

As Grace climbed into bed her mother read her a calming tale. As soon as Grace appeared to be asleep Mrs Lowing headed towards the door. She leaned out to turn the handle, but it was too late. She peered over her shoulder to see her young daughter. Grace was sitting up in bed, her eyes so wide and bright. She was just staring straight through her mother as if she was not even there.

"Jesteś martwy," she screamed. "Jesteś martwy," she repeated. "Jesteś martwy," she wailed.

"Mummy, mummy, mummy. Can we please go to the boot sale, pretty please?" begged Grace and her brother, Billy in unison.

"I've always wanted to go!" stated Grace.

"As have I!" wailed Billy.

"Well, if you two would really like to go...." said their father.

"We do, we do!" interrupted their children.

".... I don't see why we could not," replied their mother.

The whole family set out in the car, excited to witness their first encounter with the boot sale. Each person was determined to find something, something unique, something special.

"Are we there?" asked the son.

"We are, we are!" exclaimed Grace.

They got out of the car and walked through the gateway. Grace's eyes automatically fell upon a beautiful china doll, propped up on a stand. It was as if it was calling her.

"I must have it mummy! Look how pretty she is!" Grace was staring at the doll. She was so absorbed in her beauty that she did not hear her mother's response. The doll had connected with her. They were linked. There was no going back.

The family left the sale, and all were successful. Billy with a steam boat, mother with a leopard skin coat, father with a stuffed stoat and Grace with the china doll now named Raven. On the way back to the car they had to walk through fields of hip high grass and corn. About five minutes into their trek the fog arose and set in, casting a thick pool of haze around the four of them. Just being able to spot their daughter, oblivious to the weather around her, her parents and Billy set off at pace to catch up with Grace. Possibly five metres out of her range, young Billy noticed something out of the ordinary. He slowed his pace to stare, trying to figure out what he was seeing. It appeared to him as if the Raven's head was turning, ever so slowly. Billy pointed, his parents' gaze following his hand. By this time the head had completed a full 100 degree turn. Raven stared at the family, and they stared at her too in disbelief. All three saw the head mouth something, something unclear, something unnatural.

A few days passed, and the family tried to put the incident in the dusky field behind them. Most things were back to normal in the

Lowing household except one thing. One thing that involved a little, young, Grace Lowing. Ever since that day at the boot sale Mr and Mrs Lowing noticed that their daughter had not been acting like herself. As the days passed they noticed that their sweet and innocent Grace was slowly transforming into something quite ugly.

The first changes were recognisable precisely two days after the strange occurrence. It was just her body language at first. She would not sit up at the dining table as she normally would but slouched, and stared out of the window.

The next morning her behaviour grew even stranger. Grace was sitting at the table simply murmuring something to herself, and whenever anyone in her family asked what she was saying, she would merely turn around and shout, "GO AWAY!"

After five days Grace returned to her usual self, and stated that she did not remember a single thing from the past few days. Grace said she seemed to recall hearing voices in her sleep, but it was all in a different language. Polish, German, Russian maybe? But of course no one believed her. Her parents were only focusing on the fact that their sweet and innocent Grace had returned ... or had she?

A week following the outburst, everything was back to the way it should be. One night Mr and Mrs Lowing decided to go out for dinner and left their children in the caring hands of their grandmother. The children played games like Snakes and Ladders and Hide and Seek. As Grace was hiding she came across a box in her parent's bedroom that looked identical to the box in which her dear Raven came. She was just about to open the box when a lightning bolt struck on the house, making the doll's packaging fall over with a SMASH. Part of the doll's china face broke off leaving the toy with only half a face. Grace took the doll back to her room and quickly hid Raven under her bed. She then went back into her parents' room and put the box back into their cupboard. Just as she closed the cupboard door she heard the sound of the front door swing open, and heard a friendly and a familiar voice saying, "We're home!"

Grace raced downstairs to greet her parents before heading back up the stairs for bed. Her mother followed her upstairs to say goodnight. Mrs Lowing came into her room, closed the door and got out Grace's favourite story. As Grace climbed into bed her mother read her the calming tale. As soon as Grace appeared to be asleep Mrs Lowing headed towards the door. She leaned out to turn the handle, but it was too late. She peered over her shoulder to see her young daughter. Grace was sitting up in bed, her eyes so wide and bright. She was just staring straight through her mother as if she was not even there.

"Jesteś martwy," she screamed. "Jesteś martwy," she repeated. "Jesteś martwy," she walled.

Mrs Lowing heard the door lock being twisted. There was no getting out. Mrs Lowing screamed and screamed but no sound came out of her mouth. Meanwhile her daughter rose out of her bed and was drifting across the room towards her mother. They stared right in each other's eyes before Grace snapped her fingers and held up, what appeared to be someone's head. The decapitated head slowly turned around and revealed to Mrs Lowing who its owner was. As soon as she saw it Mrs Lowing realised that the head actually belonged to her! What had this creature done to her daughter and what will it do to her?

Mrs Lowing was truly petrified. She fainted and did not wake until the following morning. When she did wake, her husband, son and daughter were at her side.

"Oh thank God," said Mr Lowing, relieved.

"I thought you were dead!" cried Billy.

Mrs Lowing didn't even give Grace the chance to speak. She stood up, held Grace by the shoulders and shouted out, "You, whoever you are, GET OUT OF MY DAUGHTER!"

Grace instantly broke down in tears and raced back up to her room. Mr Lowing was so confused all he could say was, "Billy, please go up in your room whilst I talk to your mother."

So Billy did just that, and Mrs Lowing explained everything that happened to her.

"It must be the doll that we saw last week. Now it all makes sense: that doll is possessed! I noticed the box had been moved in our room it must be because Grace took it," revealed Mr Lowing.

"We must destroy that thing. Whatever it takes we must destroy it!" exclaimed his wife.

So one night they did just that. Whilst their daughter was sleeping, they snuck into her room and found the hidden doll under her bed. They took the creature outside and with their paranoia took everything out on that doll. They spent all night smashing it with bats and anything they could get their hands on, until only wire, the doll's eyes and some damaged clothes remained. Mr and Mrs Lowing hand in hand walked back into their house just in time to escape the looming torrential storms. But as they close the house's front door, the fragmented doll emerged. It stood up and screamed,

"Jesteś martwy, you are dead!"

The Man with
No Face

by Rory McAdam

The man with no face, no name and no story just wanders around the village staring, remembering the old days, how it used to be. Mum said not to talk to him. She said he's been through too much and seen too much. She said that he used to be different before the war, before it all happened. She said he was a nice chap, always having a laugh, but that was before the accident. You see the sad but true reality of war is that noone ever comes home, not really. Mum said they go out there to fight for glory where there's none to be found and that the only people coming back are survivors. They always live in the past with their fallen friends and comrades on the traumatic battlefields, reliving every moment of terror, not being able to close their eyes or rest because those old memories will always come flooding back.

There are hundreds of these men. Men with no faces across the country, all the same. All are thinking, all are remembering and all are missing. When I look into his eyes I see nothing. Merely a white washed canvas with flickers of blood. This man is unrecognisable in his ways. There is a story there that lurks behind those eyes. A horrifying story of the time he spent in the trenches, holding a dying soldier, a familiar face, a friend, in his arms whilst the guns blazed and bombs destroyed and the flames devoured, just a few yards from his weeping eyes in the once peaceful green farmland.

Anisia Fedotova

Needles

by Lilli Walsh

As the nurse walked in, her face looked sharp, cold as a block of ice, but the second she made eye contact with me, her expression softened to a beam of beautiful sunshine. She hurried about the room, grabbing syringes, plasters, anything she might need to perform a blood test. As she leant over me, wiping my arm with antiseptic and plunging the point of the needle into my arm, I could smell the unique odour that was hers. The nurse smelt of sharp, sticky blood on the surface, but underneath there was the sickly sweet smell of marsh mallows, combining with the rose perfume that was mostly worn off now but still detectable, tickling my taste buds lightly. Her swift movements and the sureness of her hands showed her experience; it was obvious she had been doing this for years.

Once the nurse (who I knew was called Andrea) had withdrawn the needle from my arm, she put a plaster where it had been.

"All done," she said softly, smoothing her scars. After a quick goodbye, Andrea and I left the room together, she to get back to work and I to get back home to my kids. She turned left onto one of the wards, whilst I turned right into the lobby. There were hundreds and hundreds of doors either side of me. I ignored all of them until I came to one that seemed to pull me lightly, compelling me to open it. I turned to look at the door, not thinking anything of it, until I saw the name on the plaque: Andrea Owens. The name echoes through my head, swirling and finally landing with a loud thump that woke me up from my daydream.

This room was the nurse's office, Andrea's office. I had to go in. I stretched out my slick with sweat, bony hand and opened the door. The first thing that hit me was the stench, an unrecognisable odour that pierced me like my mother's glare. My eyes registered the actual horror of what I was seeing. A John Doe, dead, in the seat facing me, a needle jabbed in his neck. My jaw dropped. My mind jumped. My soul turned in my stomach. The next thing I heard was the clock ticking, begging me to leave the death of this room. The drought of sun and happiness here was numbing, stripping away my humanity, piece by piece. I turned around, intending to leave the worst depression of my life and forget what I had seen there.

Luckily the nurse was not angry with me as she dragged me back to her office, but instead had an eerie calm about her, almost as if she were some sort of emotionless monster. She pulled me down onto her one and only chair, which was still occupied by the dead John Doe and handcuffed me to my chair. Once again bustling about the room, this time with the devil glinting in her eyes, she pulled out the sort of injection that you would never intentionally take. I could see from the face of John that this was what happened to him too. I was going to die. Death was swimming around my body, gloating at me, dragging me into the darkness that was giving up. Death could have been right by my ear. I believe I heard him whispering in the pop of the plastic cover coming off the needle.

As it penetrated my skin, my heart started to slow. Myra was five. She was dancing with me, moving to the beat, moving her feet in sync with mine, laughing like a hyena as she did so. Ryan was three. When I got home he leaped into my arms, so excited to see me that his eyes started to swell up and he started sobbing which made me cry with him. Sadness, heartbreak and loss melded with joy, love and excitement. This is what they mean by your life flashing before your eyes. Thousands of memories, each making the person I am today, filling me up like a petrol tank. Today was the day I was going to burst and that is what I knew in the moment. Even as death's seductive breath touched the side of my cheek, I did not waver in my newfound strength. Even as the poison's numbing puff bounced off my breath, I did not stumble or fall. I stood strong until I could hold on no longer and the black abyss beckoned me.

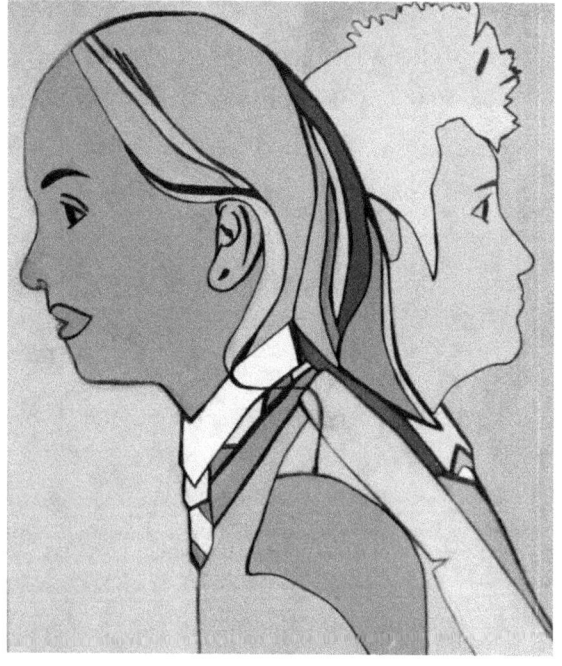

Jenna Coleman

Sides

by Gabriela Adamczyk

It is a really nice day. I feel slightly empty though. Lonely I would say, but that is okay. I am waiting for somebody. The meadow I am wandering on is vast and gives the impression of infinite. I can't see its end. There are no trees, no bushes, just short grass and tiny flowers, which in some inexplicable way makes me feel calm, very peaceful. Colours are extremely bright and the Sun, shiny smiling from the sky gives me a nice warm sensation on my cheeks. I have to smile. I close my eyes, but it feels like if I opened them. There is no darkness. I see more now. I don't understand at all. I am able to think so clearly, in this moment, every question I have ever asked, has its answer. And I am just waiting. Maybe it's boredom, that makes my mind go deeper inside its own corridors. I try to remind myself what happened, from the very morning I opened my eyes, but... I don't know. Or maybe it would be better to say, I do not care anymore. That makes no difference whatsoever. Now is important. Not how I got here, but how I am here. Exactly. How am I? I am a creature aware of its own consciousness, I have the ability to think, and I use it. I feel alive, more than ever. I know so little, but I can feel the purpose. Everything makes sense, everything has its place, everything is good how it is. I am happy, but this is just what people call it. It is way more than just a word. I make several statements similar to those, while strolling through the soft carpet of nature. I am not going anywhere, I am just moving. The real journey has its place inside, where nobody else but me, can see it. It's very unfortunate, or maybe not, that I do not have a watch… How long am I going to be waiting here? Where is she? I'm slightly nervous, I haven't seen her in ages. Will she recognise me? Will she still love me? Will she…   Somebody approached me from behind, blindfolding me with their hands. Quick analysis. Soft, tiny hands. The smell of her hair. I can't describe the feeling, it's all over my body, seven years, seems so long. But nobody knows how long it actually takes, until they experience it themselves. I turn around, see her smiling, I hear her laughter. I am looking into her eyes and so is she. My hands, touching her hands, my forehead pressing on her forehead. I tell her how much I missed her, she is not answering. She just keeps holding me tight, probably as tight as her weak, delicate arms allow her to. I put my hand to her cheek, it's wet. She is crying. Why are you crying? I don't ask, but I'm wondering. "Don't worry, from now, we will always be together. From now, you are mine, forever. Every single second, I'll be by your side. Nothing is going to hurt you. Please, look at me."

She looks. I see her tears clearly. I feel the tension inside me, I feel I am close to start crying too. I am holding her chin, move it upwards, so I can kiss her easily. I close my eyes and now, the frozen time is no more. The time is not a thing now. I feel her lips on my lips. They are wet and… What is happening?! A wave of pain bending my helpless body. I do not feel anything beside that. Where is she?! I do not feel her touch anymore. I try to open my eyes. I see nothing but distorted, wry shapes, blurry picture, I cannot say what it is. I am scared. And here comes another wave. It feels like every single cell of my body is set on fire. It is even worse than the first one, my head is filled with weird scenes, weird things, I can't describe any. Am I dying? Is this how death feels? I hear noises, but they do not mean anything, that scares me out even more. I am cold, I am incredibly cold and lonely. I feel every single piece of my body and every single piece is in pain. The pain is not passing away, it's still here, side by side with me, but I think everything is becoming clearer. I try to open my eyes again, I hear my heart beating very quickly, adrenaline fills me up to the brim, and what I see now, it's brightness. But not the brightness I saw before, not the warm laughter of the Sun. This brightness is cold. It is cold, and disturbing. That kind of brightness that makes you feel uneasy. I keep my eyes open, and I try to understand the voices. It seems like they are speaking to me. They are very loud, maybe even shouting, but I still can't figure out what. I am too cold, and too tired to be bothered with that. I just ignore them, and observe, the painful process of death. My vision is getting better, I see some creatures standing over me. The place is white, they are all white, the brightness is still overwhelming. They are talking, they seem calmer than a second ago, I would even risk saying, that they seem happy, happy that I'm with them. I keep looking at them and what I see, they are humans. Humans in white clothes. I've never been so confused before. I give up. I close my eyes and I do not even try to understand anymore. The only thing I can think of is how I promised her I'll stay forever, and I left. Now, I miss her more than ever. "That was a good job, doctor Davis, we succeeded, we brought him back to life." I hear that, and without thinking of the meaning, I fall asleep exhausted.

Jenna Coleman

Roses

by Eska Beeforth

There is an hotel, not too far from the centre of London. People say not to take the elevator. They say a lady once went in and never came out. They say that the ghost remains in the hotel. That's what they say. Nobody really believes it. Still, noone ever uses the elevator.

"Mum we are not staying up there. Not at that hotel!" Lily gasped in horror. "You know what people say! Please can we not go there, Mum?"

"It's only a rumour, darling. Besides, we could all do with a family trip away. It's the nicest hotel I could find."

Lily's mother was in truth a little nervous herself, but she insisted they went out of town for a few days, as a family, to explore the city of London. The hotel was in the perfect location.

They arrived late at night. The entrance doors swung open. Everything inside was neatly placed. As Lily and her family walked towards the grand staircase, Lily noticed that the elevator doors were glowing. The gold bars on the doors were lit up and lights were flickering. Strangely, there was a strong smell of roses coming from the elevator too. She knew it was nothing, so she tip-toed up the stairs. The next day, Lily and her family went out into London for the day.

By the time they arrived back, night had fallen. The hotel was quiet. Very few people were in the lobby. Her family walked quickly up the staircase, but Lily lingered. The beaming light that came from the elevator flickered yet again, but she tried to take no notice. She wandered along the corridor. Everything was silent. A distant rumble of thunder sounded. She looked again at the beam emanating from the elevator. As she looked closely, the flickering light started to change shape. The previous light coming from the elevator appeared now to be a ghostly figure. There was the strong smell of roses.

Lily was confused. Was it her imagination? Was she too tired?

"I don't believe in ghosts, it isn't possible," she said to herself. It has been a long day. Her family would now be sitting comfortably in their room. What was she doing standing here? Why didn't she just join the others?

Looking again, the ghostly apparition had disappeared. She returned to her room and after a few minutes, Lily fell asleep.

The following morning, as Lily awoke gently, she knew something strange had happened. Her family were nowhere to be seen. Lily knew that they had probably gone for breakfast and would be back soon. She stumbled towards the exit door of her hotel room and as she stepped onto the landing she felt as if eyes were watching her every move. She could smell something there, outside the door, something very familiar. The doors to the elevator opened. She recognised the sweet smell of roses. Lily stepped inside.

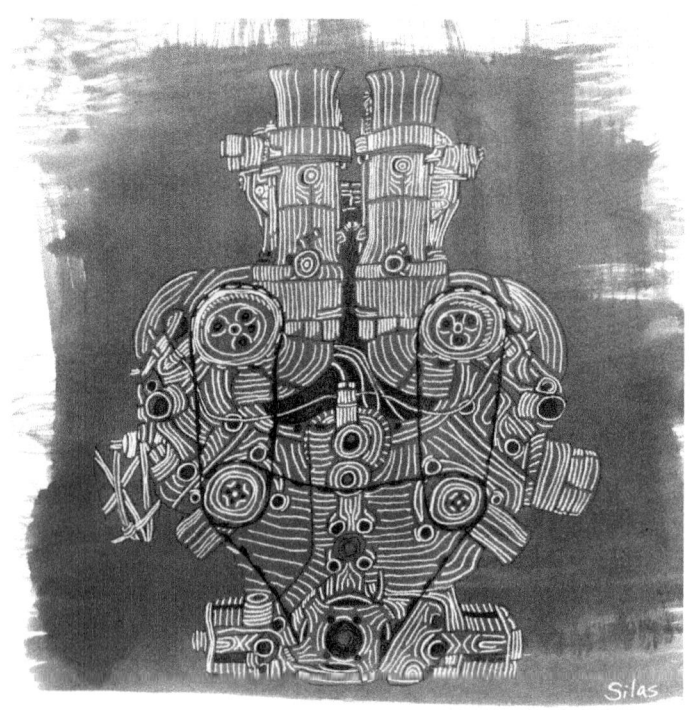

Silas Venus-Haslett

Slipstream

by Archie Robinson

"Energy. How do we get it?"

"Well sir, obviously now we get it from slipstreams."

"Correct, Toby, and who controls the slipstreams?"

"The Dominion, sir."

"And why does the Dominion control the slipstreams?"

"Because they are the only ones who can be trusted, sir."

"And who says they are the only ones who can be trusted?"

"Well... The Dominion says so, sir, and the Dominion is..."

There was a knock at the lecture hall door. Professor Steele walked slowly to the door and answered it. On the other side was a large man, who said something inaudible to Professor Steele. The professor looked puzzled and stepped through the door, following the man and did not come back in. We all sat there for about half an hour, until a thin, wide-eyed woman walked in, and said, "It seems Professor Steele shall not be joining us for a little while. Please continue you studies individually," in a voice which hinted at something indescribable.

The next day, Toby picked up a newspaper which was on his desk. He quickly skimmed through it, put it down, but then picked it back up again. There hadn't been anything about Professor Steele, which surprised Toby, as PN14 was a small town and the local newspaper would normally pick up on the tiniest of events and turn it into headline news, but there was nothing. He thought about this for a second and then decided to go to Professor Steele's house and see what he could find out. But upon arriving at the house, Toby noticed something peculiar. All of the windows were boarded up and the door had a symbol consisting of three horizontal lines going through a circle: the symbol of The Dominion. Toby approached slowly, looking around him for any signs of danger. It was well known that matters of the Dominion were not to be meddled with, or people could very easily disappear. In the early days of the reversion people had often tried to interfere or fight The Dominion, but they would always be gone within the week and all their belongings destroyed. It was clear to Toby that Dr Steele had been doing something that the Dominion had not agreed with, but what it was, was a different question. He opened the door slowly and slipped through the door, closing it behind him. Everything was left as it should be and on the kitchen table were several sheets of paper all splayed out and covered in complicated diagrams and formulas and hanging from the ceiling was a ring covered with wires and tiny white spheres and going through the ring were three beams of light which seemed to hum and vibrate slightly in the air, occasionally sending smaller crackling beams of light to one of the spheres. Every time one of the beams hit the spheres, it would glow and a dial connected to the machine would go up. Upon closer inspection, Toby realised that the dial was in fact a volt meter. It was a slipstream: a somewhat crude one, but a slipstream at that. So that was why he'd left the lecture. They had known he was doing something, but they needed solid proof and when he was asking the questions about the Dominion's control over the slipstreams, they had dispatched him immediately.

His first thought was to destroy it. That was what he had been taught. Anything that threatened the absolute control of The Dominion was to be destroyed by any means, even if it meant sacrificing your own life. He reached over for a rolling pin left on the table and readied himself. Then a thought occurred to him. What if he didn't have to smash it? What if he didn't have to do everything The Dominion told him to do? What if The Dominion was wrong and they weren't the only ones who could control the slipstreams? He dropped the rolling pin and heard it clatter to the floor. He stood there not moving, with wide eyes. This realisation had affected him in ways he could not describe. It wasn't just a realisation that he didn't have to destroy this machine: it was the realisation that his entire life was built on lies. Then a sudden thought occurred to him: he was dangerous and The Dominion would want him dead, but now that he had had these thoughts there was no way he could go back to his old life. Toby didn't know exactly what to do, but he knew he had this machine. And he knew this machine could make him dangerous. He glanced around and then went closer to the machine and studied it closer. He would have to move it to a safer place, or it would be destroyed in a few days, so he found a bin bag in a drawer and put the machine into it. The bag was extremely heavy, but at least there was no chance of the bag breaking, because they were Big Barry's Finest, apparently able to hold one hundred tons before breaking, but even with Big Barry's Finest, there was no way he would be able to even move it by himself without breaking it, but he couldn't just go around asking people if they wanted to help hide an illegal slipstream with him. Whoever he was talking to would probably kill him before he'd even finished his sentence. It was a difficult situation and one he had been indoctrinated to avoid all his life. He was going to have to resort to different means so he left the room and looked for something to carry the bag with. Eventually he found an old trolley and managed to haul the bag into it, but it was very old and the wheels were seizing up. It would have to do.

They Had Still Not Come For Me

Maeve Sutterby

Walking through dark streets at night was not my forte, but it was something I found myself doing more regularly. It was the same route I took every evening, so the pitiful amount of light emitted by the streetlights made no difference to my sense of direction.

They had still not come for me.

Everything was the same, completely normal. As I walked past, the park benches were still grotty, with chipped paint and various scars from over the years. Etched initials, cigarette burns and spent chewing gum littered the surface of the seat, making it highly advisable to avoid sitting on it. However, the missing planks of wood and the especially dark night would make that difficult anyway.

The gloom hung over the park like a bad smell. Masking the moonlight and making visibility deteriorate further, it swallowed the entire area. The air was made thick by this new-formed gloom, which took its effects upon my eyes and lungs. Even my walking was affected, as all I could make out was a crude outline of the path ahead, washed with grey.

As I drew nearer to the turn in the path, leaves still littered the ground, rotting and writhing in puddles on the tarmac. The collage of brown, scattered across the ground, drained any remaining colour from the night, leaving behind a monochrome world. But even this was normal: after all, it was mid-autumn, and the trees in the park were rejecting their leaves- banishing them to the ground.

One thing, however, that was not the same and definitely not normal, was the hooded figure now standing at the end of the track. I was used to seeing people on this walk, but it wasn't him that was threatening: it was the gleaming gun he clenched in his hand, and the menacing smirk that was wiped across his face.

They had come for me. I turned to run, but it was too late.

Mooney Wright

by Asia Koter

Let me tell you about the fantastic world of Moony Wright. Moony Wright has purple eyes and long, tangly fair hair. Yes, she washes it. She's just as hygienic as the next girl. But she spends an irrational amount of time on the Moon Hill, staring at the stars, and the Moon, and the Universe in general.

She likes to lie on the grass with her head among the heathers. She often finishes her day coming back home and being questioned by her Grandmother.

"What have you done to your clothes? What is wrong with your hair?"

She keeps on asking the same questions although she knows the answer perfectly well. She knows about Moony's loony habits, but she never approves nor disapproves of them. Gran Virginia is very introvert. She keeps her thoughts to herself. Although Moony often feels that Gran Virginia disliked her. But Moony likes to keep her thoughts to herself too. If Grandma doesn't like her, she doesn't have to. Moony is fine with it. As long as she can stargaze, she's alright.

Moony Wright lived on Lavender Cnoc, in Waterford. Lavender Cnoc was a special place, just as Moony Wright was a special person.

Of course, Moony was a bit different from other children. But before all the things that happened in this story, you really couldn't accuse Moony of being anything more than just a crazy girl who lived with her Grandma on a hill.

Lavender Cnoc was special. You could feel it once you got there. Although it wasn't a place frequently visited by people from the 'outside'. It was usually just Moony and Gran Virginia, practically all the time, just her and Gran Virginia. Maybe this is why the events in this story turned everything upside down.

A new guest arriving at the Hutch could have interrupted the status quo of the hill and new things started to happen. A new period began in Moony Wright's life and nothing was ever as it used to be.

The day began just the way it always did. Moony Wright woke up, saw the Sun high up in the sky through the skylight in her attic bedroom, and got up to get ready for the breakfast that Gran Virginia had surely already prepared.

Moony lived alone in the attic, if you didn't count the spiders and rats and perhaps other little animals. She was also often visited by seagulls, as the ocean was not far from her house. She could almost see it from one of her windows; the rest of them were facing the forest. She had a perfect view over the neighbouring hills, the most important of which was to her what she called the Moon Hill.

Moon Hill received its name many years ago, when Moony discovered the charm of staring at the sky. She was about six years old (now she was awaiting her twelfth birthday). Knowing nothing about the Universe, she could barely distinguish stars from lighthouse lamps. Before she climbed the Hill for the first time, she had never seen the Sky from such proximity. And there was one thing that enchanted her so utterly that it made her remember that day forever: the Moon.

Ever since, Moony had climbed the Hill almost every night to watch the flickering stars and observe the ever-changing phases of the Moon, looking out for falling stars and dying stars. She also climbed it during the day to watch the greatest yellow dwarf star of all: the Sun. But her favourite time of the day was unchangeably the night.

Christie Radford

Two Cities

by Sophie Ferrer

The odour of rotting fruit and festering flesh fills my nostrils, suffocating me as I wander aimlessly through this decrepit, crumbling city that in my mind is the equivalent to hell. My thoughts meander independently of my feet, and I can't let go of the feeling that something is missing. I can't place it exactly, but it's a feeling that follows me around like a shadow, like the moment before you summit a roller coaster, or the feeling you have in the few moments between flipping off your light and diving into bed at night. It's an ever-present chasm in my stomach that's impossible to shake.

Snapping back into reality with a start, I glance around to discover where my calloused, bare feet have carried me. But it's the smell that reaches me before the sight - the sharp citrus scent almost completely disguising, the sinister, underlying smell of ammunition. I know where I am now. The edge of the city, atop a hill overlooking them. Them. Those who live entirely different lives to us. In a different city, with different rules, and different morals. Complete opposites to us and yet. Something jerks and yanks and tugs me to the barrier that is the only thing preventing me from leaving my city and starting life afresh. Instead I grip the cold, unrelenting metal until my knuckles whiten. I desperately peer through the gap, unsure though of what I am looking for.

Suddenly something catches my eye. There's a slight shift in the shadows surrounding Dubuque. Someone is moving, running. Away from Dubuque, towards Solon. Towards me. People around me begin to notice, but amid the confusion I catch a glimpse of her face. I'm sure it's a 'her' now. The lightning blonde hair falling in waves on her back. Something inside me jolts. It's like the last puzzle piece has been slotted into place and I know she's what is missing. She is the hole I haven't been able to fill for years. Even the thought of her, despite not knowing her name, who she is, or where she is going, brings me to think about the beauty of magenta sunsets, the smell of summer rains, the sound of endless laughter but mostly the feeling of contentment. It's then that I decide: I need to find her.

Without thinking I'm fighting the barrier, desperately, kicking and pushing off anything and everything to give me a boost. My heel finds walls, shoulder benches, torsos, everything, willing my body over the fence that imprisons me here. In a blur, I'm over the fence, tumbling and rolling down the hill towards the girl with electricity cradling through her hair.

I've lost sight of her but I sense she's not too far away. After continued searching though, I start to panic. Where is she? I couldn't have imagined that she's real and very close at hand too. Momentarily I pause to collect myself. Inhaling deeply, I pick up the ominous fragrance of silence that can only mean impending doom. I barely processed this thought before the world erupted in an ear-splitting cacophony of noise that rips through the peace. Bullets. They're shooting at us from the watch tower in the middle of the barrier around Solon! I'd often seen guards patrolling the place, never knowing this was their job: disposing of runaways, of rebels. Dropping to the mossy floor, I consider my next move. I have to find the girl. I haven't figured out why but I just need to. Without warning a slim wrist darts out from nowhere and takes hold of my upper arm, pulling me to safety I assume, but still I thrash like a baby bird starved of oxygen. Then a hand clamps over my mouth and drags me upright. I spin quickly to face my assailant but am stopped dead by the sight of her. Time slows down as I take her in and forget how to breathe, even though the bullets are growing ever nearer. For a second I allow myself to drown as the world slips away and memories flood my mind. I know this girl. It's all coming back now. I remember everything.

Twelve years ago, the government wiped everyone's minds, stole their identities and split us into two cities, never to meet again. But here we are and the wall that binds my memories is crashing down. Tears sting my eyes and all that matters right now is that I've found my sister.

Silas Venus-Haslett

Where is Emily?

by Calli Walsh

There's always been a rumour about that house. They've said, for hundreds of years, that whoever lives there dies, but always when they were children. It must be rubbish, though, because the last woman who died in that house was old.

Emily Bennett had just turned 12 when she and her parents moved in. The house was just inland from the coast of Scarborough, in a deserted, old village, up a long stone driveway. The first time Emily looked up at the tall building, she knew she wouldn't like living there.

The Bennetts had only been in the cold, damp house for a few weeks when they started renovations. They made the house look homelier inside and out, but even after the update, Emily was still wary. Whenever she went to bed, she would hear faint noises from above her room. She thought it must be the new plumbing. Her mother said it would soon wear off.

But on one of the darkest and wettest nights Emily had ever seen, she was lying in bed trying to sleep when suddenly, in the middle of the dark night, there was a crash. Emily jolted upright in a heartbeat. Her heart was racing and thunder was ringing in her ears. Then suddenly the noises started faintly. At first she didn't take any notice, but they just kept getting louder and louder until she couldn't bear it.

Emily crawled out of bed and crept up the hallway to where the stairs led to the attic. As she was tiptoeing up the stairs, she was still trying to block the noises out of her head when they stopped, suddenly, exactly when her foot touched the top stair. She turned to face the bookcase that was standing tall beside her.

She didn't know if it was her mind playing tricks on her, but she could hear singing. It sounded like a little girl; it was a sweet voice. Then suddenly silence, no noise at all. She could see something peeking out from the side of the bookcase. It looked like a door handle, so Emily being her curious self, heaved the heavy bookcase out of the way, and sure enough, a door stood in front of her. Her hand touched the handle, but she hesitated to turn it. She plucked up her courage and the door creaked open.

The room was a nursery. Emily took one step inside and it was like stepping into a black and white world. The grey darkness turned to black as she slowly took a few more steps into the room. She squinted and could make out what she thought was a wooden rocking chair. She could also see an unmade bed with bright white linen sheets. Although frightened, she took another step towards the bed and pressed her shaking hand on to the mattress. It was warm to touch. This room was almost as if someone was living in it and looked like it had been freshly cleaned; there was no dust or spider's webs anywhere.

Emily felt a sudden gust of wind flying past her shoulder. She was hoping that it would just be a draught and turned her head slowly. Then the rocking chair started moving, rocking slowly at first and then more rapidly, and her head shot round to look at it. The darkness grew blacker and then she saw a glowing figure standing at the opposite side of the room. It was a young girl, grinning at Emily. She was wearing a white pinafore and a black bow in her long white hair. The girl murmured something as she swiftly moved towards Emily. Emily tried to back out of the room, but the girl threw her hand up and the door slammed shut. She lifted her hands to Emily's head and she fell to the ground, while the figure drifted out of the room freely. The darkness momentarily lifted, as Emily's eyes closed shut, then fell back to black as the door closed and locked behind the girl.

The next morning Emily could not be found; her parents looked everywhere but she was never found. A stillness settled over the house... until the rocking continued.

Clementine Bentley

The Other Side

by Phoebe Russell

I sit inside, watching the house, and staring nervously through the door. Waiting for an outburst I feel is to come. I cringe at the sudden sound of a leaf scraping past the window on the other side, the side overflowing with fear and darkness. My mind is telling me to calm down, but it is not that simple. Every gust of wind, every branch that falls, even the simple drips from the leaking tap put me on edge. So, calming down for me is not an option.

What did I do to deserve this? They're the ones who should feel this way. They should be the ones dealing with the guilt and the pain that is currently etched into my gut. I was only the driver. I committed no sin measurable to the others, and yet, this feeling will not subside. The memories keep rushing back. I attempt to imprison them into the mind-set that I struggle to keep under lock and key, dreading the next time that key self-turns, freeing the monster I have tried to keep inside. Only a few people have ever seen that side of me, the side I am far from satisfied with.

Now I am glaring at my own hands and images of the event rush into view. They said that we only did this for revenge, but these morbid feelings still seep their way around my body, travelling through all of my arteries and veins. I feel the emotions crush my heart for a mere second, before restarting their journey. I feel bilious. I have never experienced anything like this before, and I hope never to experience it again. I am a wreck, curled on the floor, trying to shield myself from my own guilt and regret.

I race past the French windows trying to ignore the distraught faces reflecting back into the house. I rush to the cupboards, sensing my anxiety begin to take over. I reach for a glass, but the shake of my hand will not allow me to grasp it. As if in slow motion, the glass shatters, replicating the worst sound I have ever witnessed. More images rush through. Out of the car mirror, I see the body ricochet off the ground and onto the pavement. This must have felt so normal to them but not, not to me. My gaze strays back to my hands. Now I see the blood everywhere. I look up and catch a glimpse of the car. The dark red liquid is there too, reminding me of the sickening events.

All alone in a house that isn't even mine, I presume the rest are celebrating another 'victory' in their sense. But I'm left here, as I said, all alone in an unknown house, still waiting for the unexpected. I hear the hint of music from down the corridor although all the doors are closed. The simple four beat rhythm is repetitious and is now on a repeating loop In my head. I try to ignore this slight distraction and go back to my grieving. The serrated glass still on the floor captures the moon's light and directs it all over the room. The moon's spotlights soon subside as a sorrowful figure swiftly blocks the only gleam of hope able to enter my heart. And I am now back to my self-blame.

Trying to sleep now is impossible. I pace along that corridor leading to the end. The ghastly images are still there, still re-running in my mind as if they are an old time movie playing on a scratched loop: the road, the gun, the shot, the blood, the silence. For them that killing was breathing. For me, the last of my hope… gone.

The door to the end is now in plain view, so my fate is sealed. I must go through. Through to the other side, the side overflowing with fear and darkness where there are no return tickets. I have to join them and face my true calling. This is it: I am now on the other side. The door opens…

Paula Hattenkerl

Elyse Winters

by Corbin Shearing

The distant screaming only spurred her on. The night sky was alive with the bright moon and its company of stars, but she spared no second to stare at the pretty sight. Her heartbeat hammered to the tune of Thunderstruck, the adrenaline and fear getting to her and forcing her to run as fast and as far as she could. Still, the screaming continued.

She was a beautiful girl with a radiant face and bright blue eyes. Her lava red hair drooped around her shoulders and down her back, billowing as she ran. She was in her late twenties, but even she did not know how old she was. Her last birthday had been her twenty-sixth, yet since then the days all seemed to roll into one long horror story, with no time for dates or celebrations, she could not recall her current age. Her father would have remembered.

Elyse was slim, which made it easy for her to jump obstacles and slide through thin spaces. Her heart and body were in good condition and she could feel herself outrun another living person every few seconds. She leaped over a fallen body. It was dead, that was all she knew and that was all she intended to know of it.

Fifteen minutes since Elyse first heard the initial screams, she was outside of the compound and running through the surrounding

177

forest. Suddenly, she felt so alone. She could hear no-one else running near her, no more snapping of twigs, except those under her feet, and shortly after she could not even hear the screaming, either because she was too far away, or because the violence had ceased. The forest was a deadly place in the new world, especially in the dead of night. Visibility was the worst it could ever be and anything could be lurking around the side of a tree. That was why it was always good to keep running; only in that way was she sure that nothing could catch her.

She stopped. Elyse felt a stitch in her stomach and air seep from her lungs. She had to stop or she feared fainting. Her body almost toppled over as she leant against a tree for balance as she regained her breath. Elyse was lost in the forest, but that was the least of her problems. Her biggest problem, was that she knew she had to get moving again soon.

As she steadied her breathing, she recollected the events that made the past fifteen minutes of her life. Elyse was sleeping, believing her slumber to be safe and for the place around her to be also. Then she heard a scream that woke her up. She snapped out of her dream and quickly got up and dressed in less than thirty seconds, all the while, she could hear a faint crackling noise from outside. She grabbed her knife and stepped out of her room and into the open. All around her, the compound was on fire, the people running around desperately trying to put it out whilst their duty was hindered and thwarted by a force of two-dozen hungry, flesh-eating, infected corpses.

The dead had begun to reanimate a little over a year ago, or perhaps it was under a year, Elyse had lost all track of dates. The infected people would become so by being bitten, then they would turn. Every time, they died. Then, they lived again. However, their new form of life made them crave human flesh, a want to infect countless others. As they did so, their bodies rotted, loosing sustenance, they would decay, but still they would walk, savagely trying to damn others to their hell. And for roughly a year, Elyse Winters had been fighting to keep that from happening. She was fighting just so that she could breathe another day.

The undead swamped the fiery furnace of a compound, tearing at the living and ripping out their insides. Elyse had tried to help, but everyone around her slowly began to run in fear. No-one believed that they could hold the sanctuary from the dead any longer, so they ran. Eventually, Elyse did too. She ran, faster than a lot of the people who had left five minutes before her. The camp was overrun in a matter of ten minutes. She spent the last five of the fifteen meandering out of there, past intestine buffets and burning buildings. She had helped three people escape narrow deaths, though it only took a matter of seconds for them to lose each other in the pandemonium. Next, she reached the woods and continued running until she could no longer.

A low, inhuman growl alerted Elyse to the growing danger around her. The raw groan seemed to be born from pain and an animalistic hunger. She immediately stood upright and spun around, her eyes darting about the trees, looking for a sign of the woodland moaner. It was so dark in the night, with the tall trees blocking out the distant light of the moon and stars. Twigs snapped, making her jump. Elyse drew her knife, her hands shaking from the rush and fear. The groan grew louder. She turned. The decaying corpse lunged at her, its rotting face falling apart, missing one cheek, and with a series of bloody red teeth. It forced her against the tree, hitting the bark with a muffled thud. She then hammered her knife up and under the jaw of the attacker. The knife was long enough to pierce through the hyoid bone, up the roof of the mouth, and into the brain. The light in the creature's eyes died.

The body dropped to the floor and Elyse stepped away from it, breathing hard and fast. She would never get used to the feeling of killing, if it could even be called that. Could you kill something that was already dead? Was it a kind of mercy to free the body from the mortal infection? Then Elyse remembered something she learnt it at school, something about enzymes and denaturing. Enzymes aren't living things, so what did they say it was called when they died? They didn't die, it was something else, they said they were denatured, that was it. Is that what I'm doing to them, denaturing the undead? It was the most reasonable explanation she had thought of, and it kept her from crumbling under a killer's conscience.

As the noises in the wood accumulated, the estranged moans, twigs snapping, shuffling of feet, Elyse decided to leave the horror show. Within seconds, she was running again. Her head began to throb under the stress and panic, but she kept her head straight and focused on the task at hand.

Another couple of minutes passed before Elyse escaped the woods and trundled out onto a country road. She made her way to an abandoned car and tried to open it, but it was locked, damning her to stay outside on the road. Further down the road she could see a small pack of five or six walking corpses. She could smell them better than she could see them, though she was thankful that she could at least see, now that she was in the open.

She sat with her back to the vehicle, hiding from the crowd and she contemplated her next move. If I follow the road, she thought, I might be able to find somewhere safe: a petrol station; roadside shop; or even a house that I could stay the night in. She looked over the car and saw that the group were not moving, this narrowed down her options of directions to run. Elyse reached into her pocket and pulled out a hair-bobble. The nifty tool had saved her life on multiple occasions, it pulled her hair back, letting her see better and fight without her long, red hair waving in front of her face.

With her hair tied back and breath regained, Elyse set out quickly and quietly down the road. She had gotten used to these kinds of stealth runs since the dead started to devour the living. She wore light trainers so that the runs were as easy and quiet as possible. She had known people to wear boots, which ultimately lasted them longer than her trainers, though it always allowed her to run faster and walk quieter than they could.

Half a mile down the road, she came to a bridge, crossing a canal. She stopped at the water and looked down either end of the boat-road. Both were dark, the water looked black and sick, much like everything else in the world. Despite this, the sight was strangely pretty and it made her take it all in. She might never see anything like it again.

"Hey, you alone?" Elyse suddenly locked onto the origin of the sound. Standing on the other side of the bridge was a living, breathing man. He looked just over six foot, maybe six foot two-three inches, either way, taller than her by a longshot. He was big, in a muscular kind of way, though he lacked the body-builder, gym-hitting vibe. He had rough, blond hair and dark eyes. He was clean shaven, which made him look more his age. The stranger wore heavy jeans and large black boots, which gave him a biker appeal. He wore a tattered blue flannel shirt and a brown, leather bomber jacket over that. On his back hung a packed blue backpack. He held his hands up sincerely, showing that he meant her no harm, but she could see the glint of a gun holstered on his belt and a hatchet hanging on the other side of his waist.

She looked at him, expecting him to be an illusion, though he was not. He tried a comforting smile. "What are you doing out here alone?" He had a strange accent, he definitely was not British. Elyse attempted to calculate his aim through his words.

"I might ask you the same thing?" She replied calmly after a few seconds. His smile twitched.

"I asked first." He pointed to her with his head, giving her the stage.

"I was being chased, by the dead," she told him truthfully, "I got separated from my group." She continued to tell him the truth, if only bit parts, not telling the stranger about the compound that went up in smoke. "I ran, I got lost, now I'm here. So, now you tell me." She wanted to look over her shoulder, to check for the dead, or if the man had company, but she dared not to, her eyes fixed on the foreigner's gun.

"I was on a supply run," his body was tense and showed no signs of relaxing, "and..." He looked annoyed at himself and a little embarrassed as he mulled over his words. "And I skidded on my bike to avoid crashing into a dead child. I – I, knew that she was dead, but she was still a child. So, I swerved to avoid her. I didn't realise where I was and I went over a hill, fell down it and into some woods. My bike was broken, I think I was lucky to be unharmed in it. But, I pulled something in my leg, I think. I was unconscious for some time, a couple hours I think. I mean, after the crash, I was alright, and I pulled myself away from the bike and put myself in a holly bush." Elyse now realised that his face had a series of sharp scratches decorating it, at least putting some kind of truth to his story. "I was out for a few hours, when I woke, I fought off some of the dead. My radio broke, so I couldn't contact my group. So, I started walking, and now I'm here. I saw you and I had to stop. I don't just look for supplies." He smiled at her again.

Elyse tried to figure the story out, whether or not he was telling the truth. He looked like a biker and he had scratches on his face, that all added up. "Let's see the radio." It was more of a command than a suggestion. He held his hands a little higher to emphasise that he was not going to hurt her, she gripped her knife as he unslung his backpack, unzipped it and pulled out two pieces of a broken walkie-talkie. If it was a lie, then it was a good one.

"I can take you back to my community," he offered her, zipping his pack back up and throwing it over his shoulders again. Elyse was sceptical, since the world ended, after a few months, people stopped being friendly to each other, either this man was an exception, or he was a very good liar.

"Why?" Elyse asked him, stubbornly.

He recognised her accent as being from the south of England, but it was soft and something within it rung a little northern. For example, she did not pronounce the word path with an 'r'.

"No-one I've ever crossed paths with has ever offered anyone without wanting something in return." The stranger shrugged, still a little tense.

"I am not saying that I don't want anything in return." He seemed a bit taken aback that she thought he did not have a deal.

"What do you want then?"

"It's not what I want. It's what the community wants. There's not many of us, I think there's nearly twenty now, and we need more people like me, people who can go out and get supplies for the group.

That'd be the deal. You come back with me, and you go with me on supply runs."

"What makes you think I can do that, handle myself like that?"

He relaxed, for the first time, placing his hands casually by his sides and letting out a friendly smirk. "You're alone, you're alive, and you don't trust strangers. That's all the skills I have." Elyse continued to watch his hands, expecting him to turn into a gunslinger at any point.

"You're trusting me. And what about my group? Would you help me find them? Those that survived?" The stranger nodded, as if it meant nothing to him.

"Like I said, there are not many of us, we could use more people. How many were in this group?"

Elyse felt stumped, she had joined her group a few weeks back, but she had never tried to estimate the numbers, in fact she had hardly made many friends in the group, except one, who had been a travelling companion beforehand. However, she knew that she could not just say one. "I don't know, it was chaos when we were split up... I don't know how many survived... If any did."

The stranger glanced down and took a step towards her, offering her a hand. "It's not your fault." She shot him a look with fire in her eyes.

"I never said I thought it was." The stranger retraced his steps back and nervously looked over his shoulder. Elyse quickly did the same. It all looked clear around them.

"Can we hurry this up?" He asked her, still nervously looking around. "I don't like being out after dark. Will you come with me?" Elyse shook her head, thinking about her old friend that she had left behind at the compound.

"No," she stated solemnly, if not regretfully, "I can't go with you." She began taking steps away from him, steps back off the bridge. "I'm sorry."

The stranger watched helplessly as she turned and ran from him. He wondered if she was scared or afraid of him, he was of her. Yet, her mystery intrigued him, and although he should have let her go, he began to walk across the bridge.

Elyse ran with a purpose, with spring in her feet. Orson had been a loyal friend to her since the infected menace spawned from its hell pit. They had not known each other before the turn, where he saved her life when no-one else could. Ever since they have both fought fiercely to protect each other, although that flame began to dwindle after an argument at the compound. The two grew distant, even though neither wanted to. She ran away from the compound without much thought to him, and she hated herself for that.

She crossed the road at breakneck speed and she ran headlong into the woodland. Her mind shut out the terrors that lurked in the darkness, waiting for her to fall and for their salivary mouths to begin feasting on her warm, fleshy corpse. Yet, she did not falter.

It took her under ten minutes to return to the burning wreck of the compound. The once safe place was now flooded with a sea of infected bodies, some burning, some not. The screams had died out now, everyone that was going to die was dead. It must have been a quick slaughter after Elyse left. Still, corpses feasted on the newly dead. They pulled at the guts like tug-of-wars. Their guttural groans were only drowned out by the crackling of burning wood.

The mass of smoke did not seem to affect the undead. Elyse had to cover her mouth with a safety rag that she always kept on hand, but the dead just bathed in the poisonous gas. They cared not for its mortal effects. Not even a single cough. However, Elyse's muffled chokes were silent in the noise of the fire and feasts.

"Orson!" Elyse cried out through cracked breath. She drew her knife and scanned the area, looking for a sign of her friend, or possibly becoming aware of where he went. "Orson!"

Her shouts attracted an elderly man with dry blood splattered across his long, grey beard. He was bold and his neck was ripped open, showing a clear indication of where he had been bitten. It snapped at her, its teeth yellow and brown. Elyse skipped backwards and out of the creature's clawed grasp. Then, turning her knife on the old man, she stabbed it straight down into his forehead, running through the skull and destroying the brain. She kicked the body off the knife and backed off out of the open.

"Orson!" She could not give up on her friend, she refused to leave him. "Orson!" Little did she realise that her anguished shouts were rising above the noise of the flames and into the eardrums of the undead. Slowly, they awakened to the sound of new prey, rising to their feet and trekking across the broken land towards the young woman's shouts.

"Or-" Just as Elyse was about to shout out again, a rotted woman pounced on her, knocking her to the floor. Elyse struggled against the monster's dead weight and held its snapping jaws at bay. Using all her reserved strength, she plunged her knife into the woman's throat and carved it upwards until it slid under the gullet and into the head. Elyse pushed the woman off her and breathed in a deep breath of smoky air, forcing her to have a coughing fit.

Whilst Elyse was wheezing on the ground, the dead approached her, closing the gap with a grim malice. Suddenly, she realised the threat and pulled herself onto her feet. Her vision became blurred under the painful stinging of the smoke in her eyes. Nevertheless, all she could see were smudged, grey faces, smashed brick walls and rising flames. She felt trapped, stuck. She did not want to die, she had tried so hard to escape the compound before, and now, since going back, she would die in it. Elyse had seen friends of hers get torn apart by the dead, their bodies turned inside out. Their screams still haunted her.

A wild pop filled the air. A loud blast that drowned out the flames. Bang! BANG! The noises became louder as the source narrowed in on Elyse's position. Through watery eyes she could see the shadows around her drop to the floor. BANG! BANG! Two more blasts sent two more corpses down for good. A miserable and haggard middle-aged man with burning clothes placed two gnarled hands on

Elyse, his mouth opening wide to chomp down on her and infect her with the vile virus. Suddenly, an axe-head came crashing down on the diseased man's skull and he was whipped off Elyse and sent crashing to the floor.

She rubbed her eyes and swung madly out with her knife. She quickly became restrained and pulled out of the fray, she was writhing and squirming the whole way out. Her mind panicked as she thought she was being pulled away by more of the dead.

"Calm down, calm down. It's alright." A strange voice spoke softly to her as she was dragged into a small house. She heard the door slam as she was sat down on a chair. Elyse cleared her eyes and looked up at the stranger. He was tall, wore heavy jeans, black boots, a worn blue flannel shirt and a bomber jacket. It was the same stranger from the bridge.

"I know that you said that you didn't want to join me. I know that. But, I wanted to join you." He reinforced the door with a spare chair as Elyse watched him with tired eyes. "You need to rest. It was not a good idea to come back here." He then kneeled next to her and checked her for any visible injuries. "I will help you find this Orson, but please, we have to wait. The fires will soon die out and the dead will either burn with them or leave. If we stay here and stay quiet, we should be good until morning."

She looked at him, her mind clouded with the horrific events. "Fine," she sighed, "but, if you're not going to leave me alone. At least tell me your name." He gave her his cheeky smile again, swift yet full of meaning.

"My name is Vegard Anderson." He smiled inwardly to himself. "I guess I was a tourist."

Elyse smiled at Vegard, finally realising his accent was Scandinavian, though she still could not call which. However, she smiled. "I'm Elyse, Elyse Winters... I'm glad you found me."

My First Friend

by Damilare Williams-Shires

I love how you can bring me things and people from all across time and spaces. I love how you let me see across and below seas, through walls and borders, up in the sky and beyond the stars.

I used to never let you get any rest. Still don't really. You've become a bigger part of my life but you've also become smaller, now I can take you everywhere I go.

I hate being told I spend too much time with you. I hate that I neglect others so I can be with you.

I can't blame you though. I need you as a friend. Everyone does nowadays.

Olivia Coates

Bluebell

By Damon Kelly

There's a harbour, off the coast of Whitby. It's been there for decades, maybe even centuries. It is made of wood, but it is still intact, with boats coming in and going out throughout the day. But there's this one boat, Bluebell, which people always talk about. There's nothing special about it; it's just an old fishing boat with the blue paint chipping and barnacles on the hull, but people say that you can see an old fisherman's ghost on it. You can see him still fishing, looking very miserable. And if you catch his eye you're in trouble. But this is rubbish, as ghosts don't exist.

Martin Cowen is a fisherman living in Whitby. He lives a happy life in his house in a village with his wife, Karen, and his two sons, Jim and Jake. Martin goes out to sea every weekend on his boat, which he calls 'Fish and Chups'. Martin had heard about this ghostly figure, but, being a very sensible man, he does not believe in such nonsense.

One particularly pleasant day, Martin decided to go out to have his boat checked. He went by himself, as his wife was busy reading Women's Weekly, and his boys were playing on the X-box. So off Martin went. He went to the local boat checker, called Boats 'R' Us. The official checker told Martin that his boat had to be repaired.

Martin told them to take as long as they needed, and he paid the money and off he went.

On the way back, Martin stopped when he heard some other fishermen saying how good the catch was. After hearing that news, Martin knew he had to go. He didn't have a boat, though, but then he remembered...the blue boat. He went up to the wooden harbour and stepping onto the harbour he felt a slight breeze. He took another step, a stronger breeze. Once he made it onto the boat, there was quite a strong wind. This made him all the more determined to set off before the storm took hold.

As he pulled away from shore, a thick fog started to roll in. The fog made Martin's skin clammy. Then, out of the corner of his eye, he saw something...a figure. A figure? No, it couldn't have been...then again...no, it must have been Martin seeing things in the fog.

Martin started the engine. He left the harbour and felt the fog getting thicker. He went out to where the other fishermen said the catch was, or at least where he thought the catch was. He couldn't see any fish, just the fog, the thick, dark fog. The fog seemed to be stirring up the sea. The water was becoming rougher by the second. He went to pick the oar up to turn back, but as he picked it up, it fell out of his hands and into the water. Martin felt as if he had no control over his body. As if the fog, now crawling over and enveloping him, was controlling him like a puppet. Martin could scarcely see. But then, he could just make out something, through the fog. A shape. Yes, a shape. Very slowly, the shape then turned around and it appeared to have a face. But then it was gone. All of a sudden, the boat started to rock violently, and then slowly sink. Martin started to panic, but he calmed down when he found a flare and set it off, hoping someone could see it through the fog.

A rescue crew noticed the flare about a minute after Martin set it off. They reacted immediately and got to Martin as soon as possible. Though they didn't find Martin, or the blue boat. The crew searched for Martin the whole night. They eventually had to declare Martin missing. As they crawled back, exhausted, into the harbour, they noticed a slight breeze, where usually there was calm. They pulled up to the harbour wall and moored next to another boat. A blue boat. The rescue crew examined the boat and found something carved into the hull. It was a list of names. The names were 'Jack Whistle,' 'Bob Osley,' 'Jonathan Gen.' The rescue crew suspected it was just previous boat owners, but then they saw the name 'Martin Cowen.'

Eve Harrison

Another Land

by Ellie Dudley

Two weeks ago, I arrived in Afghanistan. The barren hills dominated the arid land creating a monotonous never-ending sea of brown. I'd spent the first 18 years of my life in London cast under polluted airlines. Feyzabad was the first time I ever saw the stars; tiny diamonds covering the sky startled the eyes of small animals. I resolved to come and see my mother when my father told me she was ill. I cared little to meet her before now, for she was there and I was here and, for me, that was enough. She was rarely mentioned and there were no photographs of her.

When I arrived, I understood the state she was in just with her face: complex, with deep creases embedded within. Brown wavy hair covered her dark quizzical eyes which did not know who I was or why I was here. My voice was barely audible as regret charged within me for never visiting before. I looked towards her with hopeful eyes but her face remained blank. It was clear to me, that this woman, my own mother, was unaware of who I was. I tried to care for my mother throughout her deterioration but with no one to translate, she thought of me as only a nurse providing in her final days. To pass the time I would explore and admire the beauty of Afghanistan: and the way the mountain range blocked the light and the stars. The trees covered the barren land while the ravenous river divided wildlife and people. The cold that froze the terrain trapped in the secrets from the outside world. I felt a sense of pride that I was part of Afghanistan. Unfortunately there was still much to Afghanistan I was yet to learn. I was ignorant to its past. I was ignorant to the struggles and didn't realise quite how unprepared I was for this country. I was yet to understand what these people have already endured and how unfinished things were.

As I walked back from the market I could sense something different. Children were lined on the streets watching their father's faces turn to smiles, hope and joy bounding off as they listened eagerly to the radio. Then something above me flashed by travelling too fast to comprehend. The noise drowned my ears as the ground shook beneath me destroying everything that dared to disobey. Everything fell silent.

Compassion

by Gabriela Adamczyk

I am a good human.

I do care.

I do think about the others.

Poor people, refugees.

I pray for all of them.

I feel sorry, for the homeless cat,

That lives somewhere on my street.

I wouldn't kill. I wouldn't steal.

Everybody is equal.

Slavery shouldn't have happened.

But I seem to forget about it,

When I sit with my plate, during lunch.

I wouldn't kill,

But meat is so tasty.

I wouldn't steal,

But calves don't really need milk to survive.

Everybody is equal,

But I love my dog more than those chickens.

Slavery shouldn't have happened,

But is it still wrong, when we are smarter?

Selflessness

I am not better than the others,

But I feel like people can't love

as strong as I can.

And this is why I don't believe,

You love me.

Because,

Why would you?

There is no profit in love.

Can people still do things

like this, just for somebody?

A day in the life of Mr Meteor

by Joseph Salt

D ear diary,
Thursday 29th November, 2025.

Today I got up as usual at 7 o'clock. Suddenly I heard a loud crash followed by a cat screeching. I went downstairs into the kitchen and my eyes nearly popped out of my head - Nipper, my cat, was flying around the room at high speed, bouncing off the walls and crashing into anything in his way. I realised at once what he had done. He had eaten all of my Hoverems. These were the superhero snacks that made me fly. Unfortunately they look very similar to cat treats!

I keep a supply of Hoverem antidote in my fridge in case of emergencies and this situation certainly fell into that category. Ducking out of Nipper's way as he whizzed past again. I grabbed some antidote and quickly mixed it into his water. On his next circuit of the room I managed to grab him and hold him down as he took a drink. Thankfully it soon took effect and he returned to normal.

Now I just had time for a quick breakfast: two eggs (one boiled, one fried), a slice of toast and four cups of tea. Then I raced upstairs and quickly dressed in my usual navy suit with a matching tie. I grabbed my work pass, phone and car keys and dashed out of the house to my car. That thing with Nipper had cost me half an hour so I was now running late. I resisted the urge to change into my Mr Meteor suit and fly. I just pushed the accelerator harder instead.

I arrived at the studio just as the breakfast news round up was finishing and they were going to the weather summary. I had no time to plan anything but knowing that we were in the middle of a heatwave and it hadn't rained for a month, I just went straight into "Today the weather in and around Sydney will again be hot and sunny. Clear blue skies and highs around 30°C. Watch out for any bush fires that this hot weather could have caused. That's all from me. See you tomorrow for more weather news." As I left the studio I realised that the weather was cloudy and grey. I clicked my fingers and the weather changed to sunshine and blue sky. I didn't get to be the country's top meteorologist by getting my forecasts wrong.

Feeling rather pleased with myself I went to get a coffee. I had only had one mouthful when my phone rang – it was my secretary and she sounded flustered. She told me that there was a huge bush fire on the outskirts of Sydney and the wind was blowing it towards the city. There was no time to lose. I took a short drive to my under ground bunker beside the Harbour Bridge. After slipping into my Mr Meteor costume I donned my jetpack and turned invisibility on. I took off and sped towards the fire.

As I approached, the black smoke engulfed me. Coughing and spluttering I emerged from the other side. Through the haze I could just see the animals trying to flee the flames which were destroying their habitat. They were also moving rapidly towards houses on the edge of the city. I didn't have much time. I clicked my fingers but the smoke made me cough at the same time so my superpower was misdirected and I only made it hotter. This was bad as it was already scorching. One more try I thought to my self. I concentrated hard and clicked my fingers again. This time I got it right and the heavens opened with a torrential downpour which quickly extinguished the flames. The animals cooled off in the huge puddles. Who cares if I get the weather wrong, for once?

Silas Venus-Haslett

A Public Loo
of all Places

by Corbin Shearing

Today is the day you die. You can just feel it in the cold breeze that seeps into your windowless bedroom in the early hours of the morning. You can smell it on your morning toast and most of all you feel it in the very ether in which you live.

Naturally, it is a day of mystery and dread, never knowing how or when, it will creep up on you, never revealing itself. It is a surprise that is never lived to cause the essence of a shock. How it will happen is a terrifying thought enough, but when is a more dreaded mindset. To constantly worry if it will be in five minutes or five hours. You are not in control.

The more you ponder the existence of this nether existence the more your time is wasted. For what is truly the point of pondering the afterlife throughout the life? All those hours wasted on a question which you will never discover until it is your time. And, today is your time.

If you knew of the means of your death, surely it could easily be averted. You could avoid all contact with the way until the day is done and surely enough you have cheated death. That is why I shall not reveal the means until it is truly necessary. I will drop it like a bomb and upon impact you shall receive and take it full force.

If you knew of the time, then you could live your life to its full until the right time came. It may be a bad time, but it does not care. However, there is no avoiding a time, yet there is means to avoid a means. Two factors in your death and only one will ever be able to stop that death from happening.

Before I unveil the tale of your demise, think. Are you an atheist, or do you believe in a god? If so what about an afterlife, an afterdeath? Do you believe in them? Think strong and think hard, because truly, is what depends on your afterlife the very belief that you will go on after life? All too much to contemplate and as I said: there is no point in thinking on it.

You wake to birdsong, a crow's mocking symphony. It is definitely foreboding ill things to come. As you awaken from your slumber an icy chill pinches the vertebrae down your spine. You feel the said cool breeze upon your cheeks and around your ears. You take a deep breath in. You breathe out. Almost silently you turn on your radio.

The familiar sound of your favourite band comes on, but then there is static. And then there is nothing. The radio stops dead and the house's power cuts out. Fearing the inevitable, you dare not try to fix the problem yourself, anything could happen. Perhaps you could call in an electrician, but then again what if they are having a bad day and wield an axe in their half berserk frame of mind and bring it down onto you? No, an electrician is too dangerous.

So, you must leave it to yourself to complain to the local council, as there is no harm in that, except from death by boredom, but with an addictive app in your trouser pocket you like your odds. But, the car is a no-go. Who knows who has tampered with it in the night? A car bomb by chance. You have your enemies, but would any go that far? Maybe, maybe they were pushed by their dodgy friends that you never thought much of.

A car bomb might be the best of your worries. For what if the crazy electrician has already gone on a killing spree around you neighbourhood and has landed himself in the backseat of your car, ready for another victim. No, that thought is too horrid to dwell on.

You could walk to the building; it is only a mile away. You are fast and you believe in yourself and your ability to outrun mad electricians. Yes, it is decided that today, your last day, you shall walk.

As you step outside you smell the moisture and damp in the air, and you look up. It looks as if it is going to rain; yes you know what the sky is thinking. You know it wants to make your day as bad as possible and a drizzle of rain will do that. With that in mind, you think, you'd better take the car.

Fortunately there is no car bomb and no backseat murderer. You are safe. You take off down the drive, cautious of every turn and twist. You never quite know when teenage lunatics with their first car might swerve around the corner and smash their cheap cars into your pride and joy and take your legs with them.

Much to your delight, you reach the council in good condition.

You enter the building and complain, and then you leave. Around every corner was a different danger, but you braved it.

On your way out you notice the sky darken and a swarm of clouds fill and rally in the atmosphere. You look up in unbelievable awe as the slow drizzle mutated into a terrible sloppy downpour. You quickly jump into the car, a metal shield to protect you from the heavens. It is your safe haven, the only place you can really be safe. You swiftly check the back seats of your car, and luckily they are not haunted.

You start to drive off, forgetting all about car bombs and other such mechanical terrors. The roads are busy and alive with cadaver machines, rushing to where they need be. You wind down your window and take in deep petrol stained breaths. The toxic fumes could be poisoning your very soul at this point, but you don't really think about that. In fact your mind is too focused on the car crazily swerving around in front of you.

It only took a moment, a brief part of your existence to condemn your entire existence. It would not be the swerving car in front of you, nor the toxic fumes, but rather the car to the back of you, now accelerating to the side of your car, and now uncontrollably jerking in your direction. With a smash it converges with your metal box and two separate entities become one for a small moment. You feel yourself and your car leave the floor for seconds and then make a barrel roll across the untamed lands off-road.

From your own wreck you spy the other car bounce into a ditch and burst into a horror of flames. You are almost licked by the heat and fiery tentacles. Carefully, you watch with wondrous eyes, there is no sign of life. It is possibly more frightening to think that it could have been you in there. The very thought of your own body burning in a metal ruin practically causes the mind to create the false phantom feeling of your own body being consumed by flame.

You know that you need to escape the twisted tomb. Yet, help is only a phone call away. Reaching into your pocket to get your phone, your body aches. Your fingers feel the cool touch of your phone. Pulling it to your face you look at it. You feel stupid to only just have realised that the phone was smashed beyond belief. You can't use it to save your life. So, you heave yourself out of the car, you feel your leg burst into a million pains. The muddy ground turns into a bog with the heavy downpour and you almost have to swim out.

Now, you are sitting in the mud with the rain hammering down on you. Perhaps you shall die of a cold, but you simply refuse to accept that. In your leg now, you see it, a huge gash had made its way down your thigh, blood oozing from the monstrous cut. You feel faint at the sight, you want to fade away now and wake up in your warm bed, all this just being a nightmare. But it is not. The cold, icy rain will not let you pass away into sleep.

Another leg is sticking out of your backseat window. My god, was somebody back there? How did they get in? When did they get in? You recoil in horror, but are comforted by the dead look and motionless feel the leg has about it. No doubt it would be the electrician.

You need someplace to shelter from the rain, perhaps to pass the night off and to await help in the morning. Aha, you see a public loo not metres from the crash; you think to yourself what a strange place to put such a building, but now is only the time to be thankful. You crawl and drag your limp body towards it. The stained white building has never looked so inviting.

You smell the all too familiar smell, one which isn't worth describing. The floor is damp from the rain outside, you hope, and the harsh winds still blow in. You find it better, but only by a fine line. You make your way into a cubicle and take it all in.

You study your leg wound, if only for a second. It looks bad, but not bad enough to kill you. In here, it seems that you might as well die from infection. Surely a public toilet is not the most suitable place for an open wound. You want to cover it with something but you know that whatever you cover the wound with, it will only make it much, much worse. So, as an old remedy, to help ease the pain, you look away from it. The pain is a numb pain, one which is rare and thwarted by the overwhelming shock that your body is trying to process. The shock hasn't taken full control of your body as its friendly neighbour takes control of you like a cruel tyrant of a dictator: fear. Fear rules every move you make now and you cannot stop it, and as a paradox this only makes you more scared. A complex so undesirable that it can never truly be tested by any science lab. Fear is not a substance of the body but more a feature of the soul.

You're vaguely safe in here. At least there is hope that you can wait it out until somebody spies the burning wreckage and dials for the emergency services. Hope is lost for the other car and the other people, but you still have it and you still hope for something better, something good to come out of this. If they get to you in time then you shall not die today. However, that subject is false as you have been given the time of your death: today. That is all you know so far. You will die before the day is up. And darkness rules in the hours past five in this winter season and darkness has already taken hold. You spent more time in the council than you thought. Six fifteen is the time of death for you; at least, that is what the police reports will say about you when they find your body.

Place is another overlooked factor upon predicting death, for if you know where then you need not worry as you simply will not go there on that day. I have already told you the place: a public loo of all places. Bit, by bit it is coming together, but the one question is: how? If you know which way you are going to die then it is the easiest way to avoid that certain death. But your means of death has been staring at you the whole time and you've just chosen to ignore it as a stupid superstition.

You don't want to die, and now you know where, you can change that. You limp out of the cubicle and across the wet floor, to the doorway, leading out into the world. Maybe, you can grab the attention of a passing car; yes it is the only way. But what if in that car is a crazed electrician, like in the back of your car!

My god, you notice it there and then. The sticking out leg that was bloodied and bruised and hanging from your backseat window is gone! You gasp in horror and fall back into the public toilet and back into the cubicle and you lock the door. Your heart pounds hard and fast, you can hardly breathe, but you try and keep it together.

Thud... Thud... Thud... You hear the heavy footsteps enter the shack. Your breathing is ceased as you do not dare to even exist in the presence of what is coming. Thud... You hear stories of people hearing a killer's footsteps but never did you think it would happen to you, like this. Never did you truly realise how horrid it would be. Hearing the feet stop outside your door you suddenly ram your legs against it.

Smash! Crack! The door is broken down by a man wielding an axe. His face is dark and shadowy, his features not there. He is huge, bearlike in manner: a monster! He rips apart the final pieces and throws a pizza sized hand towards your neck; he drags you out and tosses you to the floor. You scream as hard as you can, your lungs splitting, but no one can hear you over the thunderous rain.

His leg, his weakest point! If you could just hit it, maybe you could escape. You try and kick it but your leg is hopelessly lame by now, blood draining fast. You hear the madman's voice echo around the room as he says the final words you shall ever hear: "I'm having such a bad day." You see the axe raised above his head and then nothing...

Satan Cuals

by Kieran Smith

To Andy's surprise as he walked in the living room, he came across a huge mound of presents all wrapped in shiny red paper. He beamed ear to ear and jumped up and down.

"Mummy, Daddy, you said I was on the naughty list and look what Santa got me!"

Andy's parents appeared from their bedrooms in woolly dressing gowns.

"Look Andy, we said that we, I mean Santa wasn't…" Guendel stopped as she saw the huge mound of presents before here. "Oh my."

Before Guendel could even stop Andy from opening the presents, paper was being thrown left and right. Ribbons were being unravelled.

"He got me everything I asked for," said Andy as he ripped open the box for a new phone.

Mark looked at Guendel. "I thought we weren't getting him anything."

Guendel shrugged her shoulders. "I didn't buy this stuff. I mean look at it. This must have cost a fortune."

They continued to watch in confusion as Andy opened each

present and his eyes filled with joy.

"I almost thought Santa wasn't going to get me anything," shouted Andy.

"Neither did we. You have been very naughty this year," said Guendel.

"I know! And that why I asked Santa to forgive me this year and I'll be extra nice next year, in exchange for a few things he asked from me. I even asked to get you a present," said Andy. "It's way too big to fit in this room, it must be outside."

Mark walked over to the window to the front of the house and his jaw dropped. On the driveway there was a brand new car with a giant red ribbon on top. Andy didn't even look up from ripping open presents. Guendel and Mark collapsed back on the sofa with blank faces, in shock trying to figure out where these presents even came from and what was going on.

"How did you... talk to Santa?" asked Mark.

"Some older boys told me how to reach him, you know, the death metal heads."

"Hey what's this?" said Andy as he pulled out a slip of paper with blood red calligraphy. He attempted to read it aloud:

"Dear Andy, I hope you enjoy the presents I got for you. Do remember in exchange for these gifts there is the price we discussed. I will be in touch later to complete the transaction. Enjoy your life. Cordially yours, Satan."

Nothing

by Archie Robinson

Cold can kill. It looked at him and he looked back. He took a step forward and it took a step back. He stopped. It stopped. He turned around and there it was:nothing. He turned around and ran at everything. Nothing. Why? Why was he here? Nothing. There was no reason. He was. He is. He will be. Was what? Is what? Will be what? Nothing. (Always nothing). Confusion is not real. (To understand, you must be nothing). He is nothing. It is nothing, but it is something. All around is nothing, so he goes to the only something he knows is something. (He takes two steps forward, it takes one step back). It moves. Which way? Every way, no way. Then he feels something. The only something he knows he can feel. Cold.Now it is next to him. He reaches out to touch it. It is too far away and yet it is so close. The feeling of cold grows stronger. Death. Though not him: it. Then there is nothing.More nothing, because the only something is gone. He is alone, but one thing remains: the cold. And cold can kill.

"By this you may be confused. This is to be expected. It is not made to be understood by ones who are surrounded by something. No, it can only be truly understood by one who is surrounded by nothing. Again this is confusing and perhaps odd and you may wonder what the purpose of this is. Why is it not instead simply nothing? Why is there something here, where perhaps nothing should be? If you are thinking this then you are asking too many of the wrong kind of question. Soon, all shall become clear. Soon…"

"How? How soon?"

"Look. You may know if you look. If you blind yourself, you will learn nothing.Open your eyes. See nothing. Only, you can't see the nothing because all around you is something, or at least what you perceive to be something. You may be deceived. You may be living a lie. What does it matter. Go."

"Go where?"

"Go. Do not ask."

"I am confused."

"No, you are not. Go."

"Stop. What is this? What are you?"

"I am you. I am nothing. You are something. I am something. You are nothing. Together, no. Not together, one."

"How? You are not me. I am me."

"I am you. I am me."

"This does not make any sense. Why are you here?"

"Why are you here?"

"You brought me here."

"No. You did. I am you. I am nothing. Look."

"Look at what?"

"Move. You cannot, can you? You do not know how."

"I can."

"No, not like that."

"How then?"

"(You are something. I am nothing. I am something. I can move)."

"I can move."

"(No) Hmm… Open your eyes."

"What did you do?"

"Look at nothing, then at something. Do you see it?"

"What?"

"The something. It moves as you do."

"Why am I here?"

"You have always been here. Now you are free."

"I am confused."

"Confusion is not real. (You are nothing. You have always been and yet you are still something)."

"What?"

"Cold."

"Ah… yes."

"What do I do?"

"Do not run. Be still. Look, it is here."

"What is?"

"Nothing. (Something). Touch it."

"What happened?"

"It is dead, although it was never alive."

"It is colder now."

"Good."

"Why?"

"You shall see."

"See what?"

"You are here. You cannot go back. You are surrounded by cold. Cold can kill."

Senses

by Lily-May Newman

Morning…Eat… Drink… Sleep…

Breathing. From his birth the conspiracy of breathing always confused George. At an early age he found the idea of breathing confusing and unfair. He could never puzzle out how so many molecules could determine so much of the world's future. This was probably due to the fact of how his parents died….

Morning…Eat… Drink… Sleep…

Sight. When he was two, George started to lose the ability to observe the enriching colours which engulfed us whenever we looked out onto the world in both his eyes. But it wasn't this which empowered him to see the darkness which oozed out of the world and the people who surrounded him…

Morning…Eat… Drink… Sleep…

Feel. From 13, the capability to touch and feel what was going on physically was forgotten. The sensation of delicate bubbles gently crawling all over his body would frequently feel like a kind of therapy, against the stealth of piercing bitterness which would come feeling for his flesh every other night...

Morning...Eat... Drink... Sleep...

Hear. The only sound which George was forced to listen to was the ear splitting continued screams which lived, fixed in his ears. The sweet tune of the blue tit, the warm sound of laughter and the chores of fireworks which sound so loyal to us, were no longer heard in his ears...

Morning...Eat... Drink... Sleep...

Scent. Now the only scent which found its way into the boy's noise was the harsh scent of rotten flesh, the kind from old decaying bodies which were left abandoned and souless. Before, his grandmother's fresh apple and bramble crumble after a Sunday roast was a fresh sensation which he would always try to find, nestle within the summer air; but now George's scent was limited to only this...

Morning...Eat... Drink... Sleep...

Dream. But only, it wasn't a dream. It was real. It was why

George was so mentally and physically wounded. Was it an accident? It was an accident that he was involved. But none of that mattered now, for it was just him. Alone. Isolated in his own cold heart, his own cold mind and his own cold dreams…

Morning…Eat… Drink… Sleep…

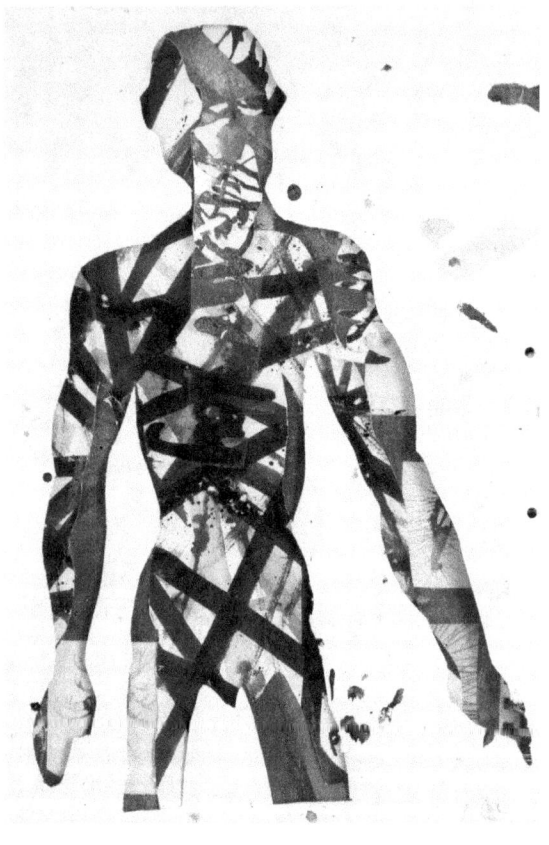

Jenna Coleman

Once the Colour Has Gone

by Maeve Sutterby

Isn't it funny how one day your world can suddenly be drained of colour, almost like pulling the plug in a bath. You don't know where exactly the colour has gone. You just know life as a monochrome screen, observing but not taking part.

You wonder if it was you that drove them away, the message you should have sent, the words you should have said, the way you always made the effort for nothing in return. The constant questioning, searching for justification. The sleepless nights concluding at 3am confusion, all a blur. Tear stained sheets and a bitter self-loathing will never make up for what they did.

You will find that once the colour has gone, you will be reluctant to let it back. Fear of the unknown. It's basic human nature: once you are accustomed to the grayscale world, you don't realise how vibrant the Universe is with its ruby red roses and other splendid specimens. Often the smallest things in life are the most beautiful.

Silas Venus-Haslett

She Jumps, She Falls, She Lives

by Milly McMorrow

I take a step back. I look down. The world beneath me is swirling like a tornado; I feel the wind racing below me trying to keep me back, away from the edge. I ignore it and push off. Falling to my death but I can't die. Not yet...

Wind and rain, lightning and thunder, a storm throws itself against the House of Usher, rattling every window, including mine. Thunder pounds the earth and the house groans.

Carefully, I carry out my bedtime rituals. Without them I would never sleep. I pad across my room to the heavy wooden door. Through the floor, I can feel the house breathing. I position the thick book to keep the door from swinging more than half open. My candle flickers. I must have the door positioned correctly before it goes out. Taking a few steps back, I survey the room. The half open door still feels... wrong. I adjust it, nudging the book with my foot. It creaks louder than a door should when moved so slightly. I rest my hand against the wood - too long, because feelings seep into me that are not my own.

The house wants me to open the door. To put the book back on the bureau, to straighten the rug. The house hates closed doors. But completely open doors are just as terrifying as being closed in with ... whatever might find its way into my room. There are things, living and dead, creeping through these halls, and I'd rather they ignore me while I sleep, as they do during the day. The house will protect me, but I feel safer with the book holding the door in place.

Lightning flashes as I turn, illuminating the empty corridor, and my path to my four-poster bed. I blow out the candle and pull the quilt up to my chin. And now, I listen. The clock in the hallway ticks away the minutes. It will chime at midnight, or upon the hour of its choosing. A sound patters in the hallway. Pat pat pitter pat, coming closer, ever closer, stopping before my doorway, and the pat pat pat over the threshold and into my room.

I don't dare breathe. I lie as still as possible, straining my eyes against the darkness. A slight shape approaches, slinking in the gloom. A flash of lightning reveals my brother's solemn face standing at my door.

"The storm?" I whisper.

"Yes," he whispers back. Roderick is afraid of everything.

"Hey, it's only a storm," I whisper.

His eyes accuse me of lying. Nothing here is just anything. This is not just a house. We have never simply been children. We are Ushers.

I try to console Roderick but my attempts fail me. A large crash of thunder and lightning startles him. Next thing I know Roderick throws his head back, and he screams until I fear his throat will be torn apart. I desperately try to calm him down, I even push my blanket to his mouth, frantically trying to stop him before it's too late.

Our mother glides into the room. She shines in the lightning as Roderick did, and is more graceful than even a ghost. I can't take my eyes off her. When she reaches my bed, she slaps me so hard that my head hits the headboard. My eyes burn but I don't say anything as she scoops up my brother into her arms and carries him away. The house whispers to me, louder in my ears than the storm outside. I lie in the centre of my bed, listening to the crash of the thunder which now comforts me. The house is to blame.

The next day. Placing one hand in front of the other, Roderick and I crawl forward through the accumulated dust of the library. Roderick points to a table in front of us and I head towards it. Next thing I know the floor creaks outside: Roderick and I exchange a look and scurry as fast as we can to sit under the nearby table. The next second my mother strides into the room shorty followed by father. They are obviously in a heated argument.

"She has to go. It's just not safe anymore. She is even starting to infect Roderick as well as you and me," exclaims my mother in a state of distress.

"We can't just kick her out of the house. It won't let you and even if it did where would we take her," argues my father. He always tries to protect me from her.

"I don't know and I don't care. She just needs to be out of this house. Or even just separated from Roderick. I can't have my darling boy turning out like her," my mother retorts.

"What do you mean turning out like her? It isn't her fault she is going to die,"

Silence. My brother and I are in a state of shock. What do they mean I'm going to die? How long have they known this? How could they not tell me? When is this going to happen? My mother calms down and softens her voice, "I know it isn't her fault but I have to make the decision for all of us. I have to protect this family."

More silence. Roderick starts tugging my arm. I know he is right. We need to get out of here. Mum will sense us soon but I can't move. Finally, he manages to drag me away but not before I hear father mention the raven's tongue.

That night I lie in my bed tossing and turning. Eventually I make the decision to go to the library and see what I can find out about this tongue. As I descend the stairs I feel the house wanting me to turn around. I proceed down the marble staircase back to the library. I'm searching for what feels like hours when I finally stumble upon an old dusty book at the back of the library. I read and read and read when I finally find out what this raven's tongue does. The book says that the tongue is in the house somewhere and it can grant one wish. It also says that there can be dire consequences but I'm not too bothered about that. I just want to be with Roderick. I must find it and I must find it soon.

By the time I retire to my room again it's dawn so I start my search. I keep searching all day and have no luck. It's about ten o'clock when my mother calls me. I cautiously meander down the stairs to the salon where I find my mother and father sitting on their chairs. My father avoids eye contact and mother just glares at me as I stand in the doorway.

"Madeline, I know you overheard our conversation this morning and I'm sure that is why you have been avoiding us all day. You need to know the truth," my mother starts in a way she thinks is comforting.

My father still avoids my gaze. I can tell he doesn't agree with this and mother is forcing him (like she always does).

"Sweetheart, I don't know how to say this but yes what we said earlier is true; you are going to die, on your eighteenth birthday. Which is only in a few days so your father and I," she kicks him under the table. He just glances at her then looks back to his hands resting on the table. She sighs, "Your father and I have had to come to a very difficult decision and you may not be happy with it but it is what has to be done." She beckons me. Intrigued but cautious I fill the space between us. She lowers her voice. "We are going to get you out of the house."

All of a sudden there is a crash outside that makes me jump out of my skin.

"The house heard you," I mumble. Still in shock from the bang and not coming to terms with this news being bestowed upon me.

"Go to your room and lock the door," my father startles me by finally speaking but still avoids eye contact. What has she done to him? He would never agree to this.

I'm dazed. My mind is whirling with all of this new information. Crash! Another bang snaps me back to the real world. I turn on my heel and absentmindedly dawdle out of the room. I don't go to my room though. I start the next part of my search. I search quietly upstairs until my parents retire to their room. Then I sneak down the stairs to look some more. That's when I hear it speak; the house. It has never actually talked to me before. It's in my head.

"The attic," it whispers to me.

Without even thinking I turn around and walk towards the attic. What am I doing? Do I really believe that the house is going to help me stay? I reach the attic and I am pulled towards the back of the room. I look in a box and find the raven's tongue. How? It's right here? I hear movement downstairs. I hear my mother ascending the ladder. I knew she was going to hear me. I glance at the now weighted object in my hand. There is a sudden ping of guilt from somewhere deep inside me.

"Madeline?" my mother is close. I can feel it.

Then it just happens.

"I wish that I can live past my deadline and break the curse," I did it. Did it work? What did I just do?

I brace myself for the hit that I am expecting; my mother appearing behind me furious. I wait, and wait, and wait but nothing.

I ready myself to turn around and I turn. No one. Where is she? I run down the ladder with the raven's tongue in my hand. I go straight to Roderick's room excited to tell him that I don't have to leave. I quietly tap on the door. No answer. Maybe he is still asleep. I peer inside and am gobsmacked as to what is on the other side of the door. His room; it's empty.

Terrified I run to my parent's room not caring if I wake anything in this house. I run straight in without knocking to find the same thing... it's empty. As if they have been erased. I run downstairs to see if they are downstairs. Nothing. I peer out the window. Nothing. I frantically search all around the house but there is no one here. There is no one anywhere. I'm all alone with the house. I'm just all alone.

I take a step back. I look down. The world beneath me is swirling like a tornado; I feel the wind racing below me trying to keep me back, away from the edge. I ignore it and push off. Falling to my death but I can't die, not yet. I just lie there on the floor, in a heap. I miss Roderick. It has been 154 years since I have seen him. I remember the last time I was with him under the table in the library. I miss father protecting me. Dare I say it, I even miss mother. I lay there, a single tear trickling down my cheek.

Silas Venus-Haslett

Goldrush

by Kieran Smith

I didn't know for a long time what father was building in the garage until the day he died. He wouldn't let anyone in the garage at all. Mother wasn't even allowed to bring him cups of tea. He kept a kettle there so he wouldn't be distracted. At the end of his life I didn't see much of father. The only times he was around was during meals where he would eat. I wouldn't see him at all when I came home from school. It would only be at dinner, where he would emerge from the garage covered in stains. I could hear nuts and bolts jingling in his pocket and he always wore a utility belt that had all sorts of tools on it. Other than that he was pretty normal. He would ask me about school and occasionally he would help me with homework. Dinner for him was always brief. He would usually gobble up his food and then go back into the garage. That left me and mother to eat alone. I don't understand how mother would have put up with this behaviour, not seeing him throughout most of the day. She must have had some idea of what he was doing or at least understood why he was doing it. I asked her nervously what he was building in there and she would never answer, leaving the dining room in an awkward silence. Other odd things would happen as well. Father had large crates and boxes being delivered to the house and he would drag them into the garage before I or my mum had the chance to see what was in them. He was clearly building something, and whatever it was, it was big.

Things have changed a lot since my dad's day. He was born in 2018. Back then things sounded really primitive, fifty years ago. Dad said it was really dangerous. I can't believe actual people used to drive cars themselves. Now we have no traffic accidents at all on our roads and flight paths. People didn't enjoy life then. They just had to work all the time, doing horrible menial jobs. People don't have to do that now as all of those tasks are done by our robots. The problem we do have though is that since robot mining and manufacturing is so much faster and more efficient, we've run out of natural resources. The good news is that thanks to some smart people, we are looking to asteroids and moons for fortune and glory. People go in droves on rockets so they can get a piece of an asteroid and mine it out. Their hope, to strike it rich with the chance of finding some gold and come home with mountains of money for their families. But my family wouldn't do anything like that, besides that kind of prospect is way too dangerous. A lot of people never make it back. Either they die or they become too greedy and decide to stay and be part of some new colony away from the Earth. Sometimes we would hear roaring coming from outside. I would always race to see miniature rockets the size for only one person to fit in launching straight up into the air until they disappeared into white hot flashes into the sky, and then we would go back inside the house as if nothing had ever happened.

Occasionally we would see some rockets launch up and then

we would watch them explode in mid air. That would happen at least once a month, always shocking to see, knowing we had just watched one of our neighbours perish in fire and flame.

I never suspected my father would ever be a part of that. I always thought he was building something for the house like a new service robot or maybe he was building something special for me like a football machine, but my suspicion grew stronger as he spent more and more time in that garage, and I became a bit older and less naive. I wouldn't have wanted my father to just leave us like that in the hopes of getting more money for our family, let alone the chance he would die in the process or decide to stay there for good.

Weeks turned to months, months turned to years until the day finally came when I found out what my father was doing. He couldn't resist that fortune. I was walking down the street from school and I saw a rather small rocket about the size of a large van. It looked rather well built but you could tell it was homemade. It had a cone shape at the top with all sorts of nuts and bolts tightly holding sheets of metal together. There were three fins planted onto the ground supporting the spaceship on our driveway, and a ladder leading up to the door of the ship which had a wheel on it to tighten the door. I saw my dad was standing next to it adding some final touches. This time he wasn't wearing his usual overalls and welding goggles with his utility belt. He was wearing a pale space suit. One he ordered from the internet. Mother was standing outside the front door watching him.

"Dad, what are you doing?" I asked.

He came up to me and hugged me. I could see tears rolling down his cheeks.

"Son, I'm going away for a while, but it's for the best," he said through the tears.

"Why? Where are you going?" I said as I nearly began to cry as well.

"I have to go and find us some gold. We need it for our future. We need it so we can get you into a good school so you can have a good future, son."

"How long?" the tears started forming.

"I'm not sure: a few years, maybe."

"But I don't want you to leave."

"I know, I'll miss you too. Your mother will look after you."

Mum had appeared behind me and hugged my father almost in tears. Father's spacesuit gleamed in the sunlight holding his helmet with a reflective visor under his arm. Mother came up to me and held me tightly as we watched father put his space helmet over his head and twisted it shut. He blew us one last kiss goodbye and ascended the ladder. He looked at us again when he swung the door shut. We stood well away from the ship as we braced for its blast. We could see him dialling in on the console through the tiny round window surrounded by bolts.

The ship made a whirring sound and a countdown had begun. He stared at us through the window. We could see that his eyes were red from crying. The booster from the ship grew red hot and we could see a flame starting to grow from underneath, charring the concrete of the driveway to go black. The flame grew hotter and hotter. The spaceship began to light up with green and blue lights. Then there was a deafening blast, the spaceship began to ascend into the air very rapidly and it left a black crater on the concrete. My face was salty from the tears as I could not stop crying. I didn't know when was the next time I would see my dad again. The ship had thrown itself into the air very steadily and it seemed to be working. For a moment I was proud of my dad and I began to understand what he was doing for me.

But in a sudden moment we saw that the spaceship had caught fire. We stood there helpless, in horror as the ship began to produce black ink smoke. Like a squid. Without a moment's notice, the ship shattered into millions of pieces. Red and yellow flames erupted in the sky and thick black smoke engulfed the remains. We could see chunks of the ship soaring in the sky making their way Earthward. Then we heard the blast. My mother broke down into tears kneeling on the porch of our house. I just stood there helpless. I didn't know whether to cry, help my mum or just look at the explosion. I just sat beside her and she cried on my shoulder. We sat there until the remains of the ship began to rain down on us like gold.

Silas Venus-Haslett

Come Forth, Two Arms

by Edward Burke

SAMUEL

Darkness. That was all Samuel could see as he contemplated the battle to come. Would he live to greet the evening? Or would the cold embrace of the pit be his last. Bitter, Merciless. Then suddenly nothing at all. He wasn't entirely sure which was worse. Whilst he pondered this fatal question a sharp point prodded him from behind. Kevin was urging him on now, or maybe it was No-nose. He couldn't tell in this accursed darkness. Nevertheless, he entertained his captors and walked forward to the rusted iron portcullis. He could hear the roar of the crowd now, yet he couldn't make out the words. The darkness was pierced by huge floodlights, like a somewhat unwelcome sun bursting through the grey of morning. His eyes were flashing uncontrollably. His thoughts were tripping over one another, as he struggled to pull his consciousness out of the melancholy pool in which it bathed.

The Announcer's voice reverberated around the chamber. Cheery, jovial, welcoming and most of all, loud. The kind of loud that pierced through your shattered thoughts, twisting, turning until it touches your very soul.

"Ladies and Gentlemen, welcome to this week's thrilling four arm fight!"

Samuel could make out the small rotund man. He was bellowing at the top of his lungs. His face was a bright red.

"Over in this corner we have the reigning champion, old slash n' bash himself, the one, the only SAMUEL."

As soon as he heard his name, Samuel stepped forward, through the now open portcullis, and raised his arms in the air. The crowd went wild. Samuel could make out faces in the crowd now. He was mildly surprised at how diverse the spectators were. There were fathers with children on their shoulders, groups of four or five women on their Friday night out, he could even see the odd elderly person coming to watch him fight for his life, old, greying, withered, but not tired of the violence it seemed. Of course, there were the ones who were there every Friday night without fail, the gamblers. There was a man selling odds and another pair who were arguing about who would win. Samuel's thoughts were broken abruptly as the Announcer resumed his unholy bellowing.

"And in the other corner we have the new challenger. Hailing all the way from India, we have Scimitar Saul!"

The iron portcullis rose and a four armed man emerged. He had olive brown skin and the makings of a beard. He was brandishing a different blade in each hand. In both his upper hands he had a pair of gleaming matching scimitars. In his lower left hand he had a cruel looking cleaver and in his lower right he had a wickedly sharp dagger. As Scimitar Saul raised his arms in the air, he smiled. When he did Samuel saw that, much like himself, his teeth had been replaced with vicious razor blades. They had spared his hands though Samuel thought. He had not been so lucky. His upper right hand had been replaced with a double edged axe blade and his lower left had been replaced with a spiked mace. He looked upon the man whom he must kill and felt only sadness, but that would not stop him. No-nose poked him from behind as the Announcer's voice boomed once more.

"Are we ready folks, this is going to be a good one, 3 2 1 FIGHT."

Scimitar Saul lurched forwards and swung at Samuel with both his scimitars. Samuel blocked the right with his axe but the leftmost flew upwards and slashed his cheek. That small flash of pain cost Scimitar Saul dearly. Samuel grabbed Saul's uppermost left arm with his own uppermost left hand and brought the heavy spiked mace down directly upon his shoulder. Saul recoiled away but his scimitar skittered into the sand. The Announcer bellowed once more.

"Oh isn't this a good one, it looks like Saul has lost his scimitar."

Samuel pressed on his advantage. His axe came crashing down and Saul met it with his scimitar. The wickedly sharp cleaver swiped down and bit deep into Samuel's thigh. Samuel reacted swiftly and grabbed his wrist with his upper right arm. He twisted violently and the cleaver fell to the floor. Scimitar Saul plunged the dagger downwards, aiming for his stomach, but Samuel was ready for him. His lower left hand fired out and wrenched the dagger from Saul. Before Saul could react Samuel stabbed the dagger into the palm of his hand, pinning it to the ground. The deafening voice boomed again.

"Oooh would you look at this. It looks like Saul's down to his last scimitar."

Scimitar Saul jerked backwards and pulled himself free. With his last remaining unwounded hand, Saul grasped the fallen scimitar off the floor where it had fallen. The Announcer roared again.

"This is looking to be an exciting finish, isn't it folks? Scimitar Saul's back in his home territory now."

The dual scimitars twirled as Scimitar Saul advanced. The leftmost blade slashed at Samuel's throat. It was all he could do to clumsily knock it away with his mace. Saul swung the rightmost blade low aiming for Samuel's legs. He jumped back as the blade whispered across his calf. Scimitar Saul swung with his left, but Samuel to his dismay realised that it was merely a feint. The right blade sliced forward. The tip of the blade cut him diagonally down the chest ruining his cotton shirt. Saul smiled triumphantly, flashing his gleaming razor blades. Samuel fell to his knees.

"Kill him. Finish him," the crowd roared.

Scimitar Saul rose his left blade into the air ready for the final blow. Samuel struck. His dagger skewered Saul's wrist and his axe swung down. The blade bit deep into Saul's elbow. Samuel swung again and Saul's forearm fell to the fighting pit floor. The Announcer shouted with glee.

"Yikes would you look at that? We ought to call it the three armed fights now."

Samuel ignored the jape and continued the fight. Saul swung his final swing. Samuel caught his arm easily and twisted it, thrusting the scimitar into Saul's foot. Saul howled uncontrollably. Samuel put an end to the infernal racket. His mace smashed into Saul's jaw and there was a sickening crunch. The jaw was hanging from a small piece of skin on the right hand side.

"I'm sorry," Samuel whispered.

He brought the mace down onto Scimitar Saul's head. There was a horrendous sound as Saul's head was crushed like an eggshell. The crowd went wild.

"Oooh what a finish folks what a finish. Congratulations Samuel, masterfully played. Next up we have the sixteen man melee to decide who fights Samuel next."

Samuel began to walk back to his entrance when he noticed just how large the arena was. Up above the pit was a solid concrete ceiling but no lack of light due to the two huge floodlights. Underneath the ceiling was a large hall like square room; however in the centre of the room was a large circular arena that was about three metres deep surrounded by iron railings. He was jarred away from his thoughts by the distinct sound of gunfire. By this time most of the challengers had entered the arena, all clad in their grisly mutilations. As No-nose turned to drag him out of the arena a bullet slammed into the back of his head, exiting precisely through the hole where his nose had once been. Kevin dropped his spear and drew a pistol; he opened fire into the mouth of the tunnel where the bullets were coming from. Samuel acted quickly and grabbed the fallen spear from the floor and plunged it into Kevin's unprotected back. At this point all hell had broken loose; the crowd was screaming and running in every direction. Some of the people had pulled out their own firearms and were pointing or shooting them at the mouth of the tunnel. Suddenly six four armed men charged out of the tunnel all shouting and screaming and shooting.

"For the Armistice, for freedom!"

The Announcer produced a small machine pistol and sprayed down at the four armed men. One of them went down in a burst of blood and glory. A dark haired four arm lobbed a grenade up where the announcer was. There was a large explosion as the Announcer was sent flying into the pit below. Samuel retrieved the pistol from Kevin's corpse and stepped over to the wounded form of the Announcer. He pointed the gun down at the Announcer's bulbous head.

"Kill the scumbag and get the hell out of here," shouted one of his new found compatriots, a large barrel chested four armed wielding a sawen-off shotgun. His only really stand out feature was that his left eye was swollen and red and leaking pus. The iris darted around as if it didn't really know where it was. His reply was a hail of gunfire. The barrel chested man seemed unperturbed by the bullets until one of them began to hiss as it flew through the air. It hit the sand in a burst of hellfire.

"Laser-Eye, get the hell outta there!"

Sweat poured down Samuel's brow. The Announcer beneath him whimpered clutching his wounded legs. Samuel wanted to shoot this man. He knew that deep down he really did.

"No plea-" Samuel slapped him to cease his begging. "You made me kill so many people, you are a monster." Samuel cocked the gun. "I ought to kill you right now and be done with it, but I shan't. You don't deserve such mercy. Do you even remember Pikeface Pete or Strongman Silas? Metal Marv, Serendipitous Simon, Conman Chris, Irvin van Norman aka the Killdeathinator and Scimitar Saul? Don't you remember all those men you made me kill? You are the scum of the Earth. I hope they haunt your dreams until the day you die." He lowered the gun.

Tongues of fire licked at his cheek. He grabbed his new found friend 'Laser Eye' and dragged him from the flames. He turned back and saw the wall of fire that blocked him from his much wanted revenge. He cursed and continued dragging. The dark haired four armed man took 'Laser eye' from him and urged him into the tunnels.

Samuel looked behind himself and saw the sixteen challengers that the Announcer had released were not faring quite so well. Corpses were strewn across the arena. There were about eleven competitors still alive only five of which were on his side of the flame.

A burst of gunfire whittled the number on the other side from six to four. The four brave men charged into the flames in a last ditch effort to escape. Three of them emerged victoriously on the other side. The fourth was not so lucky. The flames clung to him and refused to let go. He ran screaming until the flames consumed him. Samuel, surrounded by the now eight remaining pit fighters, began to run for the tunnels when without warning a bullet thudded into his shoulder, knocking him to the ground. He drew his pistol and returned fire. All of his shots missed. The gambler who shot him however still died as a bullet pierced his head. To Samuel's extreme dismay he saw that the men who had slain him were all members of the T.A.I.S (The Auxiliary and Infiltration Squad). They aimed their special guns that had dangerous interchangeable ammunition. Samuel broke into a sprint as they opened fire. He watched in horror as a man to the side of him went down in a burst of flames. He was at the mouth of the tunnel, seconds from the entrance, when the bullet slammed into the back of his knee. With a cry of pain he spun into the floor. The other seven men ran past him out of sight. The T.A.I.S jumped down into the arena to give chase. It was at that point that Samuel knew all was lost. He would die today. Then the dark haired man ran into his vision. He opened fired on the secret policemen striking one in the chest. Whilst this was going on Samuel realised that this particular four armed man had a particularly severe mutation. One of his fourth arms jutted out from his neck rather than his side as was the norm. It was with this arm that the man leaped upwards and grabbed the portcullis bringing it slamming down. With their entrance blocked, the three T.A.I.S men simply drew their guns and opened fire. The dark haired man reached down and pulled Samuel to his feet. As Samuel was half walked and half carried away, bullets flew all around him. One such bullet hit the ground with a hiss; strangely this was a different hiss than earlier. Samuel soon found out why as lime green fumes swirled through the air like deathly spectres. The dark haired man produced two dirty rags from his pocket he pressed one onto his own face and clamped the other on Samuel's. He began to speak to him through the muffled rag.

"Hi, the name's Nigel, Nigel Greene. You're a tough guy ain't you to come through all this. So what's the name, tough guy?"

"Samuel," Samuel whispered through parched lips.

Finally Samuel saw the light at the end of the tunnel. Together they limped forward to the light, forward to the Armistice, forward to freedom, forward to the unknown...

JAMES

Jimmy hated school. St Wolfgang's was situated just a half mile away from the nearest four arm ghetto. This ghetto was the dump that Jimmy Watson and his sister Sally lived in. Right now Jimmy was in an incredulously tedious maths lesson doing nothing but counting the minutes until the bell rang. His hidden arms ached like hell, but there was nothing that he could do but grin and bear it. He looked behind him and mouthed a word to his lifelong friend, Mikey. Mikey was an extremely sanguine guy. He loved nothing but a laugh and a good time. He was Jimmy's link to the world of popularity. All the guys thought he was their best friend and all the girls swooned over him. Most importantly he had only two arms. The same could not be said for Jimmy. Whilst he did enjoy a good laugh now and again, he liked to think of himself as a deep thinker. Additionally he was what teenage society considered a nerd. He had an extensive collection of comic books that he loved to read. He even went to the schools meagre board game club. Of a whopping 2,400 children that attended St Wolfgang's, only two (occasionally three) other boys went there. The teacher who ran the club was a teacher whom Jimmy had a great appreciation for. His name was Mr. Irvine and he was the best teacher to grace the school, no the world, with his easy going presence.

"James Watson, must you daydream every lesson. What have you actually written down?"

"Uuh, x = 5."

"Dear God, boy. Must you strive to such utmost levels of incompetence every lesson."

"Um no, sir, not every lesson."

"Detention tomorrow after school. Failure to attend this will result in a day of isolation."

"Yes, sir, sorry, sir, it won't happen again, sir."

"Oh but it will, won't it James?"

"Yes, sir. I would like to apologise in advance, sir."

Mr Dawson opened his mouth to talk when without warning the bell rang. The children surged and Jimmy followed suit leaving mathematics behind. Mikey walked next to him.

"Right mess you got yourself into there, isn't it, old Jimbo me buddy."

"Shut up; as if you can talk. You've had as many D.Ts as me, Mr. Popular."

"Now that is extremely debatable, my misfortunate friend."

"What have we got next?"

"It's lunch, you fool."

"Are your words always this scathing?"

"Nah, they're normally worse, but you caught me in a good mood."

"You are an utter scumbag. You know that, don't you?"

"So what did you do for half term?"

"Absolutely jack all, as per usual. How 'bout you?"

"Not much, just a few low-key parties."

"You're having a laugh. Your parties are never low-key, and you know it."

"Very well, you've caught me red handed this time, Jimmy."

"Anyway, what are you having for lunch?"

"Just school dinners. How about you?"

"Dogfood sandwiches as usual."

"Gaah, how can I say no to that? Alright, I'll buy you your lunch."

"Thanks, Mikey. You're the best."

The duo arrived at the lunch hall. They found an empty table and Jimmy sat down at it whilst Mikey left to get lunch. Jimmy sat there in silence for about ten minutes before a familiar hand tapped him on the back. It was his sister, Sally.

"Hey Jimmy, rough day, huh?"

"Suppose you could say that."

"I hear you got a detention today."

"Indeed I did."

"Oh come on, Jimmy. What was it this time?"

"Mr. bloody Dawson and his stupid maths lessons."

"For crying out loud, Jimmy. What will Ma and Pa think?"

"How am I supposed to know?"

"Jimmy, it's time you grew up."

Sally got up and left. Five minutes later, Mikey sat down with his hands full of food.

"Here's your cheese chicken and pesto toastie and your

strawberry whip."

"Thanks pal; I don't know what I would do without you."

"Ah don't worry about it, I've got no problem with buying you a dirty pesto sandwich."

Jimmy said something that was uninterpretable due to the vast amount of food that was in his mouth. Mikey grinned.

"Come on, Jimmy, that's pretty grim. You're dripping pesto all over the place."

As if on cue a large blob of pesto slopped onto the once pristine table. Jimmy quickly polished off the rest of his sandwich. Mikey was still half way through his cheese and ham toastie.

"Cor, you made a right mess of that, didn't you?"

"Shurrup. At least I've finished mine."

Jimmy took the lid off his strawberry whip. Mikey's face twitched in sheer revulsion.

"If the sandwich was grim, that is utterly vile. I mean that gloop hardly constitutes as food."

"Simmer down, it's tasty as hell and a lot better than you could get in my entire village. It was hard to pretend that his ghetto was a village in the middle of nowhere and not a dung heap just outside of town. Yet it wasn't nearly as hard as hiding his extra arms from all his peers. Mikey was the only person in the entire school save Sally who knew. Jimmy had just finished his whip as Mikey started on his cookie.

"You really do take your time eating, don't you?"

Mikey replied by producing a pair of headphones and placing one into his ear. Jimmy was bombarded with the voice of Leonard Cohen singing.

"I like to take it slow I've never liked it fast, for you it's got to go, for me it's got to last!"

"Bloody hell! Can you not listen to anything but Bob Dylan or Leonard Cohen?"

"Sure I can, I also listen to Strawbs, Genesis and Pink Floyd."

"I seriously cannot understand your strange taste in music."

"You mean my excellent choice of music, do you not?"

It was so hard to argue with Mikey, because no matter how much you disagreed with him you just couldn't help but like him. Just as Jimmy began formulating his next sentence the bell rang.

"Oh hell, I've got to run. I've got hard ass Hilton."

Mikey swiftly ran off. Leaving Jimmy on his own once more. The rest of the school day went without incident. Jimmy, Mikey and Sally walked past the Pearce dry cleaners on their way to the local ghetto. Jimmy could clearly make out the striking auburn hair of the owner, Josephine.

"Oh Jimmy fancies Josephine!"

"I do not," Jimmy said indignantly.

"Come on Mikey, leave him alone why don't you?"

Whilst the teenagers were laughing and joking, a small non-descript white van pulled up just a hundred yards ahead of them. A smiling man with four gold teeth got out of the van and walked towards them.

"Uh guys, I don't like the look of this," Mikey muttered.

"Nor do I."

The man with the golden teeth was on them.

"Hi kids how are you. Do you want a lift?"

"No, we're fine."

Sally tried to walk past but the man grabbed her by the side and all hell broke loose. Sally's blazer tore open and her extra arms revealed themselves. The man with the golden teeth pulled out a rag and clamped it on Sally's face. Within seconds her body went limp. A second man, who had dark skin, emerged from the van and sauntered towards them. Mikey turned around and broke into a sprint. Jimmy was all alone. Thoughts raced through his head. He wanted to run more than anything. But he had to save his sister so he charged into the dark skinned man with all his strength. He swung his fist at the man's head but he ducked and returned the favour. The powerful fist struck him directly in the temple. He collapsed. As he was falling to the floor he saw the man with the golden teeth hurl Sally into the van. His head hit the concrete, and everything went black...

GRAHAM

The streets of New Kensington were cold and dark. Graham walked warily, his hand on his holster. He walked past a bright pink neon sign of a scantily clad woman and his lip curled in distaste. He walked ever so slightly more briskly. He had an informant to meet. Sean Phillips was a man of ill repute; his file was peppered with petty thefts and misdemeanours. There was even the odd mugging. Yet just recently his partner, Johnny Krillman, had received a tip off saying he had some information of extreme importance. Johnny ought to have been here but he was in hospital after being shot in the raid on the fighting pits.

A blood curdling scream pierced the night sky. Graham ran to the source of the sound and saw that a young woman was being harried by two men. One wore a hoody, the other a hideous torn vest. Graham drew his gun.

"Kneel down and put your hands on your head."

The man with the torn vest reached down to his waistband and began to produce a gun. Graham switched the dial to cartridge two and fired twice. There was a loud electrical buzz as the man lurched and his limbs jerked around before he collapsed to the floor unconscious.

"Holy crap, it's the T.A.I.S!"

The man with the hoody broke into a run down the alley behind him. Graham switched the dial to cartridge nine and fired six times. Each bullet hit the man with a thud and a scream. He fell to the floor in a wailing heap. Graham strode over to where he was and grabbed him by the hood. He dragged him to his feet. He pulled back his sleeve and sure enough there was the tattoo of a roaring demon.

"Tell me what you know about Roaring Rory and his gang."

"Clyde Phelps ain't never gonna grass on Rory. Its more than my life's worth."

"There is going to be a lot of pain in your immediate future if you don't tell me where his is."

"Screw you, law dog. I ain't telling you nothing."

Graham grabbed his arm and began to twist.

"Where is he?"

"Go to hell!"

There was a crunch as Clyde Phelps' ligaments tore and his bone snapped. He howled in agony.

"Last chance. Where is he?"

"All right, all right I give up. Him and his gang is at The Illustrious Blonde. They've got some guy with him. He don't look like much I don't know why Rory wants him."

"See that wasn't so hard."

Graham slapped him with his gun and he fell to the ground with a thud. Graham pulled out his radio and pressed a button. The radio crackled to life.

"I need a pickup squad at my current location. I've got two perps; one could probably do with a medipac, over."

"Pickup team is on bound, over."

"I could also do with some back up. I'm going to take Roaring Rory down, over."

"There are two officers on patrol in your vicinity, sending them to you now, over and out."

Graham arrived just outside of The Illustrious Blonde. This place was a real sleazeball. It would be hard to find a more sordid establishment in all of New Kensington. Graham turned and saw that his back up had arrived. One of them he recognised, a potbellied middle aged man with fiery red hair who went by the name of Sgt Mcleod. The other man was clearly a raw recruit. He was fairly tall and had light brown hair and an easy going smile. Graham could even see that he had braces on his teeth.

"Hi I'm Gerald Young. But Sarge calls me Young'un."

"Good to have you, Young'un."

"It is an honour to meet you, Captain Jones."

Mcleod chimed in in his Scottish drawl, "So what's the plan , cap'n?"

"Do either of you have thermal goggles?"

Young'un produced a pair of funny looking glasses. Graham put them on and looked into The Illustrious Blonde. He saw a total of twenty three heat signatures. Eight of them were scantily clad dancers and one was the cook. It was the fourteen armed men that worried him. Nine of the men sitting in the clubs tables were merely thugs but the other four were Roaring Rory himself and his three underbosses, Tattoo, Sharkface and Simon Wyman. In the centre of it all was Sean Phillips.

"Hell, this is not going to be easy."

"Why what's in there?"

Graham told them and together the three of them laid out a plan. Half an hour later a man and a woman stumbled into The Illustrious Blonde drunk out of their minds.

"Well well well, what do we have here?"

It was Rory himself who spoke.

"Who are you?" came the reply in a heavy Scottish accent.

"The real question is who the hell are you?"

The pair had wandered into the centre of the club by now.

"Ah well that question is much easier to answer. My name is Sergeant Mcleod and you are all under arrest."

Mcleod drew his gun and fired at a thug with a number one cartridge. He went down with a grunt of pain. Simultaneously two bullets hissed through the air. Lime green fumes filled the room. Mcleod and the woman pulled gas masks over their heads. Graham and Young'un charged into the room. Young 'un sprayed the thugs with bullets and two of them collapsed. Tattoo and Sharkface charged at Mcleod. Sharkface's shark like face contorted in rage and he bared his filed shark like teeth. Mcleod was actually worried; right up until Graham fired a number six cartridge and his head exploded in a burst of blood and brains. Tattoo slammed into Mcleod and they both went down. The dancers all ran out to the back door whilst the cook walked into the room wielding a cleaver. Graham shot him before he could do anything stupid. Simon Wyman and three of the thugs ran towards an overturned table but one of Young's bullets punctured a thug's lungs and he fell to the floor mortally wounded. This was a dangerous risk as the other four thugs opened fire on him whilst his back was turned. Three bullets thudded into him and he fell to the floor. A pool of blood began to form around him. He raised his gun and fired at the thugs killing one of them with a bullet through the heart. Tattoo drew a long bronze knife, pressed a button on the hilt and swiped at Mcleod. The Scottish sergeant could feel the intense heat as the blade whispered along his chest.

"Damn, he's got a heat knife!"

"You're gonna die, pig!"

Tattoo slashed again and the blade sliced into McLeod's cheek melting the flesh. Mcleod screamed in pain as Tattoo closed in for the kill. Graham holstered his gun and drew an experimental electro knuckle duster. He slid the rubber section onto his hand and charged at Tattoo. His fist struck the gangster with an electrical crackle. He turned with a grunt. The huge tattoo of a roaring demon that covered his head seemed to come to life as the brute charged at Graham. Tattoo hit him, with the force of a raging Colchis Bull. Tattoo was on top of him, the blade raised ready to kill. All of a sudden Mcleod swung a chair into Tattoo's head and he collapsed to the floor unconscious. Mcleod pulled Graham to his feet. Graham barked an order.

"You take those three. I've got Wyman."

Mcleod turned to the thugs his face a portrait of pure rage. The thugs broke and ran. Mcleod shot one as the other two ran out of the club. Mcleod followed them out. Wyman and his men fired from behind their makeshift barricade. Graham returned fire. The bullets all hit the table and ricocheted off. Graham surmised that they were reinforced so he switched to cartridge number five and fired at the table. The bullet pierced the armoured table and through the spine of a thug. It continued deep into the floor. Before Wyman could register what was happening Graham switched to cartridge number four and fired at the exact same spot. The floor behind the table erupted into flames. As Wyman and his thug fled Young'un fired stun bullets at them and they fell to the floor. Graham turned and saw Roaring Rory holding Sean with a gun to his head.

"Surrender or he dies, copper."

"He dies you die."

"Uh can we not talk about me dying, please?"

"Shut up!"

Graham glanced at the dial on his gun and saw that it was four places away from what he needed. He lifted his second hand onto the gun, one finger on the dial.

"Drop the gun or he dies."

"Drop your gun or you die!"

The dial was on explosive now. Only two steps away.

"I ain't dropping my gun, you smug son of a bitch."

Just one step to go now.

"You've killed your fair share of people, Rory. You deserve to die more than most."

"You ain't going to do it, pig!"

The dial was at number eight. Graham pointed the gun at Sean and removed his finger from the trigger to signify that he was not a target.

"Whoah what the hell are you doing?"

Graham lifted the gun and pointed it at Roaring Rory's head. His finger pulled the trigger slightly. His trap was ready to spring.

"Last chance Rory, surrender or die."

"Die!"

Rory pointed his gun at Graham when he pulled the trigger. Roaring Rory died as he lived: bloody and gruesome. Graham's bullet flew through the air nimbly dodging Sean as it burst through Rory's throat. After it had exited it turned in the air and pierced his black heart.

"Holy crap, that was too close."

Graham noticed what was happening far too late. Tattoo had awoken from his slumber and was on top of Young, his heat knife raised. Graham hurriedly fumbled with the dial trying to switch it to number two. Gerald Young feebly raised his arms in defence but Tattoo swept them aside easily. The knife plunged downwards, aiming for his heart. The knife blade met his flesh with a burning sound.

Graham fired.

The bullet hit Tattoo in the neck and his limbs jerked sending the knife flying across the room. Graham ran to Gerald and knelt beside his unmoving body. He looked down and realised that he was too late. Gerald Young was dead; the knife had cauterised his heart. Graham looked down at the recruit and did something he hadn't done in years. He wept. Mcleod burst into the room with his two captives in tow.

"Is he alright?"

"He's dead, Greg."

"He died well though, he died fighting for a reason. This entire anti-four arm gang is going down and that son of a bitch is going away for a long time."

"It is my fault, if I hadn't called for backup; if I hadn't brought him along he would still be alive."

"If you hadn't called for backup you would be dead."

"Maybe that is what should have happened."

"Um excuse me, is it alright if I interrupt?"

Graham stood and wiped his eyes.

"No it's not all right."

"Come on Graham; let the man talk. It's him we're after any way."

"Why did Roaring Rory want you?"

"He found out about my little brother Shifty Shaun."

"What the hell are you on about? If you're pulling my goddamn leg I swear you'll..."

"Woah! Woah, Woah. No need to be so hasty, cap, I ain't lying to you."

Mcleod intervened.

"Listen here, boy. Enough of that stupidity. Speak it all and speak it true."

"I am. You see my twin brother Shaun is what Rory was after. It's the entire reason he was gunning for me."

"What's so special about your twin brother."

"Well you see, he has four arms."

Graham, astounded, starts to rejoin the conversation.

"So your telling me that you, a two arm, have a four armed twin brother?"

"Yeah and his name is Shifty Shaun, what about it?"

"How the hell is that even possible?"

"Don't ask me. But it's true."

"So, Rory wanted to kill you because you are associated with four arms?"

"Kill me. Nah Rory wanted me so that he could use me to contact Shaun."

"And why would he need to contact Shaun?"

"Ah, well. Shaun has gone undercover."

"Where?"

"The Armistice."

Mcleod's fiery eyebrows arched in amazement. Graham rubbed his tear stained face and stood back.

"That, that's huge."

"You're not putting us on, are you, boy?"

"Shifty Sean never lies."

"Your name makes that less believable."

"Don't judge a book by its cover."

"Has anyone ever told you how annoying you are?"

"Countless times, my stubbly friend."

"I'm not your friend, boy."

Mcleod chimed up.

"Can we stop with the foolishness, boy. Can you contact your brother… Shaun."

"I can try, but what's in it for me?"

"You can't try, you will, boy you hear me?"

"You sweeten the pot or I'm leaving right now, Captain Jones." Mcleod again.

"Listen boy don't be so hasty. How about we add in a full police protection for you and your family as well as a new placement in district 11D."

"This guy is a much better bargainer. That sounds good. I'll go contact him now. Meet me here at half one tomorrow."

Shifty Sean placed a crinkled note into Graham's hand and with that he slinked away into the shadows. Graham was left with just Mcleod and the unmoving bodies on the floor. He unfurled the note in his hand and saw the location. 117 Grungham Street. Dumbfoundedly he handed it to Mcleod.

"Any idea where that is, Greg?"

"Not a clue. I guess we'll find out tomorrow."

"You mean, I'll find out tomorrow. I'm doing this alone."

"But..."

"I need this, Greg."

Mcleod raised his hands, defeated.

"You're the boss, boss."

"Damn right I am. You deal with the paperwork on this one, will you, mate? I need an early night."

"What do you mean "early night?" It's half one in the morning."

"You know what I mean. You can deal with this, can't you? See that these four go away for a long time."

"Yeah, of course I can. You look after yourself, Cap. I'll see you tomorrow."

"Likewise, Sarge."

Graham opened the large mahogany doors and entered the cold dark night beyond. He wandered aimlessly for about an hour and a half just brooding and contemplating the events of the night. Young'un's face kept flashing into his mind, his cold dead eyes piercing Graham's very soul. His nightly walk stopped briefly as he passed by an off-licence, Booze 'n' Bits He stopped outside, feebly attempting to suppress the urge to enter. He failed miserably. The store clerk greeted him amiably.

"Hey Graham, bit early aren't you?"

He grinned his stupid grin. Graham was in no mood for this.

"I'll have the usual, Sangit."

Sangit bent down below the counter and produced two six packs of Hobgoblin Beer. Graham's favourite. The logo was stupid, but the beer was good.

"That will be £16.92."

Silently Graham produced a twenty pound note and waited, seemingly an eternity, for the change, then left. The cool night air brought out goose pimples across his skin. Soon he would be home, ready for another sleepless night filled with regret and remorse. He arrived at his crummy apartment block, fumbled for the key, fiddled with the lock and then entered. He was greeted by the ever-familiar poor attempt at air conditioning. With both packs of beer in his left hand he pressed the elevator button, waited restlessly and got in. He keyed in the 57th floor. The doors closed behind him. They opened too soon. He exited, turned left then walked to the end of the corridor before reaching apartment 211. He once again fumbled with the key before he was greeted by the welcome sound of the lock clicking. As soon as he entered he was assaulted by the pungent odour of rotting food and unwashed clothes. He entered the kitchen first, opened the fridge, retrieved a Ginsters Cornish pasty and put it in the microwave. After the perpetual 3-minute wait, Graham devoured the pasty like a wolf would devour a deer. Fully satisfied, he retired from the kitchen and opened the bathroom door.

He brought the beer with him. The wait for the pasty had already dropped the number from 12 to 10. His first port of call was the cupboard above the sink. He produced a frayed blue toothbrush and a tube of toothpaste. He brushed his teeth like a man possessed. The harsh bristles scratched at tooth and gum alike. When Graham finally spat out the sink was crimson. He looked up at the mirror and saw that well over half of his teeth were dripping with blood. He uncapped a bottle of Listerine and took a swig. His mouth burned, but it was a good burn, a clean burn. Not like the one he had given that four arm in the pit. He spat the mixture out. Still the green was peppered with red. Dissatisfied Graham began to run a bath. He poured in the bubble bath, too much really. But he did not mind. He would have need of all that soap. To wash away his sins. He stopped the bath when it was half full and scalding. Graham undressed and entered the bath. He winced at first, but it was all right, pain was good, pain was real. Surrounded by bubbles Graham popped the cap on his beer and began to glug. It was after his third beer that he came up for air. He thought about Young and his molten heart and that four arm he turned into a human candle, hell, even those thugs he gunned down. By now the tears were streaming down his face and his sixth beer of the evening was sloshing down his throat. The seconds turned to minutes and the minutes to hours. Graham looked down at his feeble form, the arms that were spindly, the belly that was too fat and the bags beneath his eyes that grew larger every night. His thoughts raced to his glory days, back when his muscles were toned, his arms like tree trunks and his face as handsome a face as you would ever see. Back before the T.A.I.S. Back when he was just a rookie NKPD cop out on his first mission. Back before the world went to hell.

Back before Martha died.

The tears were welling up once more and Graham let out a heart wrenching sob. How long it went on for he could not say. Too long. All he knew was that it was on his eleventh beer, with the hobgoblin grinning down at him brandishing his axe, that Graham Jones Captain of the T.A.I.S finally closed his eyes and sank deeper into the bath with beer bottles and bubbles floating all around him.

JOSEPHINE

These were the people that she was born to despise but somehow, in some way she could not. And so, she would not. All she felt for these people was pity and a stern sense of altruism to see her through. As the mutilated four-armed men began marching out of the tunnel and into her laundry shop she was horrified at the sheer violence of it all. There were violent gunshot wounds and macabre pieces of half rusted metal sewn onto the flesh of these downtrodden people. Where her ancestors, even her father, would have whipped them she would comfort them. Where her father would starve them, she would feed them. Where her father would freeze them, she would shelter them. Where her entire line would enslave them, she would see them freed.

Seisor greeted her at the end of the solemn procession. General Seisor was a cautious man, but of course he had to be to run a rebellion. Whilst there were other rebel leaders, anyone who knew anything knew that Seisor was the heart and soul of the rebellion. Seisor was also a tight lipped pragmatic man, occasionally taciturn. He was not a man to be trifled with. He wore a dark grey wide brimmed hat, a long black trench coat with four arm holes, and had freshly shined black loafers. His eyes were cold and seemingly unfeeling, but Josephine knew that this was false. He hid great compassion and kindness behind those cold dead eyes of his.

"How many did you save?"

"Fourteen all told minus the man we lost, Reggie."

"Why have you only sent eleven to me?"

"You have keen eyes, Miss Pearce. Two of them were strong enough to train with us as is."

"And the other?"

"He would not come."

"What do you mean he would not come? Did you tell him what this place is?"

"Yes, and he refused."

"Why on Earth would he do that?"

"He said he did not need our help, though he begrudgingly allowed Nancy to tend to his wounds, of which he had many."

"Madness, sheer madness."

One of the men broke off from the crowd and approached the pair of them. He had a rat's nest of dark brown hair that looked filthier than most rats' nests. Other than that he looked unmutilated and unhurt. His eyes kept darting around as if he was looking for something, but didn't quite know what.

"What's all this about madness?"

Seisor was the first to reply.

"Nothing you need worry yourself with, boy."

"Sounds mighty worrying if you ask me."

Josephine could see the annoyance begin to grow on Seisor's face. She interjected before anything stupid could happen.

"Listen, kid. If you must know we were talking about one of the men who refused to come here."

"I almost envy him. He didn't have to go on a long ass walk just to end up standing around in a freezing cold basement."

Seisor's rage boiled over.

"Why you insolent ungrateful little wretch, I just risked my life and my men's lives to save your sorry carcass from a life of imprisonment, mutilation and death. And you repay that kindness with whining and moaning over a bit of cold. I ought to have let that announcer have his way with you."

"Woah woah, simmer down big man. I don't know who you think you are."

"Who am I? Who am I? You audacious cretin. I am the man that you owe your entire life to."

"Uh um can we just?"

He raised his voice for all to hear.

"I General Seisor of the Armistice am the man you are all listening to. I'm sure you've heard about me in the news. The man who defied the two arms, the man who built the Armistice up out of nothing. I don't ask for much from my men but respect and loyalty would go a long way."

This time noone dared speak. Seisor continued.

"Don't for one minute think that any of you are being forced to stay here, safely hidden away from your would-be captors. Any man who wishes to may leave now and go back home to their slum to live a life of squalor and captivity. I will not stop you. But any man who stands his ground now and stays will live a life of honour and glory. He will fight against oppression and adversity. Fight against the T.A.I.S and the anti-four arm gangs. Fight against the two arms. I cannot promise you freedom. I cannot promise you wealth. Hell, I cannot even promise you survival. But I can promise you this. You will live or die for a cause. You will live or die for the Armistice. You will live or die so that your children and grandchildren may one day live in a world where all mankind is equal no matter how many arms they were born with."

This time he was met with applause. The crowd began to call out their praises.

"Seisor!"

"Freedom!"

"The Armistice!"

"Hail Seisor!"

Josephine could not make out who had said that last one but smirked in approval anyhow. She stared at the man stood there in front of the crowd of men he had just won over and could not help but admire him. Ever since she met him she always had a profound sense of admiration for him, for this man who had turned up out of nowhere and became a legend. He had built the Armistice from nothing and instantly grew himself an extensive reputation. He had won countless battles and skirmishes against the T.A.I.S seemingly knowing what they would do before they knew themselves. He struck hard and fast and always slipped away before reinforcements could arrive. He was renowned for just how few men he lost in his daring raids. Perhaps the most astounding thing about the enigmatic man standing before her was that he still managed to be a kind and benevolent leader who ruled with a warm heart and an iron fist. Yet there was something about him that Josephine did not like, something eerie, something he was hiding. Maybe it was the way he looked whenever he gave a riveting speech, maybe it was the fact that she nor anyone else had ever seen him in anything other than what he was wearing today. Was it really him?

Still she spoke for him. He could have his secret so long as he was in charge the revolution could not fail, would not fail.

"Now that Seisor has said his piece you may make your choice. Follow me to join the Armistice or follow him to go home to your slum."

For once, no one followed General Seisor. Josephine let out a small sigh of relief. Seisor pulled his hat across his face, turned and walked back into the tunnel alone. A smile was painted across his face. Josephine watched his shadow disappear into the tunnel. Once he was out of sight she pressed a button near the wall and the tunnel mouth sealed shut leaving just a brick wall once more. She turned to face the new recruits.

"Seisor wasn't lying when he told you that this is technically your rest period. But I am fairly sure that he refrained to tell you that this is no cake walk. You will be up each morning at the crack of dawn working and readying yourselves for your training."

"What training?"

"Were you not listening to the General's speech? You are going to be revolutionaries not boy scouts. So yes there will be training. And in the state that some of you are in you aren't likely to survive it and some of those who do will no doubt die anyway. Is that sufficient information for you?"

"Your half-cracked lady."

"You'll be half starved if you don't shut your mouth."
She led them along the basement floor towards the "mess hall" and the "barracks". They stopped, and she opened a door in the brickwork wall. Inside was an impressive array of bunk beds. At the end of the rectangular room was a door that Josephine knew led to a toilet.

"This is where you will be for the majority of your stay here."

"Don't seem like much if I'm being honest."

"There is a common room across the hall and a gym down the hall."

"That's not too bad I suppose."

"All right well I will leave you to your new living space. Dinner is at seven in the mess hall. It's my own homemade shepherd's pie."

"That actually sounds pretty nice."

"Oh it will be."

With a curt nod she swiveled and left, heading for the stairs. Whilst she was walking she thought about the events of the past few months and still couldn't quite believe what had happened. Meeting Seisor, joining the Armistice, hiding four armed stowaways. It all seemed so unreal, so distant. And to think that she, Josephine Pearce the daughter of a large and powerful slave owning family who had used four arms for their own benefit for generations, was part of this revolution against the corrupt and blind government. It was almost too much for her to handle. Almost. No matter how terrified she was of being caught, she could not explain how good it made her feel to help these helpless impoverished people, to defy her family. The basement and tunnels that they had built all those years ago to smuggle slaves into the household were at last being used for good. A loud tinkling bell rattled her into her senses. Someone was here. She hurried upstairs, anxious to find out who was there. Had she been found out already? She reached the top of the stairs and smiled with equal parts satisfaction and relief. It was just a customer coming for his weekly dry cleaning.

"Can I be of assistance, sir?"

"Yeah I just need these suits done for Wednesday."

"That's fine. Let me just take those for you."

He draped the suits over onto the counter. She picked them up and looked at the material, checking to see which cleaning process it would have to go through.

"Heard the news lately?"

"No what's going on?"

"The T.A.I.S have raided some four arm fighting pit."

"Oh how awful."

"Yeah, I mean those four arms are everywhere. We'll never get rid of them."

"Tell me about it. Who knows where they'll turn up next."

NIGEL

The Twenty Pin Bowling Alley was an absolute uproar. Laser-Eye and his cronies were shouting and preaching some nonsense or other. Probably about mounting a suicidal charge against the T.A.I.S. Laser-Eye was a strong man and good in a fight but other than that he was an absolute idiot. The fact that Seisor had chosen him as his lieutenant still astounded Nigel. Whilst Nigel did not like to self-aggrandise he was the better choice, both more loyal and more cunning. The wits were just a bonus.

"Death to two arms. I Laser-Eye believe that we four arms are actually superior to the two arms even though we are persecuted."

"Yay Laser-Eye!"

"Down with two arms!"

Trouble was brewing. Nigel could feel it, could feel it tingling in his bones. A storm was coming. He had to put a stop to it.

"As much as I support our leader, I firmly believe that we should strike the two arms now whilst they are unaware of our plans. For the Armistice!"

"Shut up, Laser-Eye. Quit running your mouth. We follow Seisor, not you."

"I'll give it to you, mutie. You sure have got some stones, talking like that to me. But let me make this perfectly clear. If you don't scamper away right now I and my boys will beat you into yesterday and back."

"You call me a mutie, but you are the real scum. Using the power Seisor gave you to belittle and bully others into serving you. Well I won't stand for this."

Nigel drew a wickedly sharp kukri blade from the sheath on his waistband.

"Looks like the freak wants to play with the big boys. Leave this one to me, lads. This is gonna be fun."

Laser-Eye produced a monstrous meat hook from his back pocket and grinned maniacally. He charged forward. A bulldozer made flesh. The weapons met. Sparks flew.

"Come on, boy. Let's have us some fun."

Laser-Eye swung his meat hook lazily. His goons began to both jeer and surround Nigel simultaneously. Nigel went for a swing at Laser-Eye's belly, when, without warning a huge fist thundered into his head. He went crashing to the floor. A giant of a man with a bushy

275

blonde beard stood over him.

"Bloody hell, Nige. What do you think you are doing?"

"Gunthor?" Nigel raised his head and looked up at the huge Scandinavian man. He had a huge beard complete with blonde moustache and hefty head of hair. Over one shoulder he had a fur skin draped lavishly. This was the only piece of luxury that he had. The rest of his clothes were plain and simple. On his back a huge Warhammer was strapped with two worn pieces of leather. Gunthor lovingly called it 'The Happy Stick.' Nigel was one of the very few who had felt its touch and lived. It was a very exclusive club. Gunthor knelt down and scooped up Nigel. He unceremoniously slung him over his shoulder.

"Excuse my idiot of a friend. He should know much better than to mess with Seisor's top lieutenant."

"He certainly should, Gunthor. Next time he won't get off so lucky."

"Sure thing, lieutenant. I'll take him to the infirmary now," with that Gunthor turned and left, heading for the infirmary.

As they were walking Nigel spoke up,   "What did you go and do that for Gunthor?"

"You were about to get yourself killed."

"No I wasn't I could have taken Laser-Eye easily."

"Exactly, once you beat him his goons would have killed you."

"Ah I see, hadn't thought of that."

"No, no you hadn't, you never do."

"I know it's just th..."

"We're here," he pulled Nigel off of his shoulder and then led him through the infirmary door.

They were greeted by Nancy, the nurse. She had long dark hair, very pale skin and was wearing a small blue nurse's uniform. There were three beds in the infirmary; two were empty and one was housing Samuel, the mutilated four armed pit fighter with weapons for hands.

"Well well, what do we have here?"

"It was my doing, miss." It was Gunthor who spoke.

"What is it this time then?"

"Nigel decided he wanted to fight Laser-Eye. I punched him before he got himself killed."

"Nigel, you lovable fool, what did you think you were doing?"

"Well, it's just that Laser-Eye and his stupid claptrap really winds me up."

"Hey, nurse, more morphine, this guy is just bitter because he wanted to be lieutenant but Laser-Eye got it instead of him."

It was Samuel who had spoken. He was now sitting upright on his hospital bed. Nancy went over to the man with a syringe in her hand. She produced an antiseptic wipe and wiped the underside of his elbow. She then levelled the syringe just above his vein.

"Sharp scratch." She plunged the needle into him and began injecting the morphine into his bloodstream. Samuel was laid back and his lip was tightened. There was about ten minutes silence before

Nigel decided to speak.

"When is lunch? I'm getting hungry."

"Fifteen minutes from now, don't worry."

"What's lunch?" it was Samuel this time.

"Today it is burgers and chips. No pudding."

"That doesn't seem too bad."

"No I guess not."

"Do I need any procedures done, nurse?"

"No just some frozen peas and paracetamol. You'll be fine. Samuel however, after lunch we will have to remove that last bullet from your knee."

"All right, can't wait."

There was a knock at the door.

"Come in!" Three four armed men walked in. One was called Mortimer; he had two assault rifles slung over his shoulder. He was a deadeye with both. Next came Lionel; he had a scraggly beard and gaunt features. There were multiple knives strapped across his body and a revolver holstered at his hip. Lastly came a hulk of a man with a shotgun on his back, a meat hook at his waist and a huge swollen red left eye.

"What the hell are you lot doing here?"

"We are not here for you, Nigel Greene. We are here to welcome young Samuel into our group."

"Wait just one minute; you can't do that. He should go through Seisor first."

"Due to Seisor's absence, I his lieutenant must take over the duties of recruitment." Gunthor spoke now.

"Well lieutenant, I know how much work I have to do now that Seisor is not here. Perhaps you could let me and Nigel look after Samuel?"

"Normally my friend, I would agree wityh you but that friend of yours has insulted me grievously. He cannot be rewarded for such dishonor."

"No he cannot, but perhaps I alone could look after the new recruit?"

"I am afraid that is not an option, Gunthor. He must be trained properly and suitably. We both know you could not do this yourself, don't we?"

"How about we let the man decide himself?"

"Very well Samuel, would you like to train with me or this… Viking?" The words were filled with a cold hatred. Samuel swung his legs over the side of the bed and gradually stood. He began to limp forward.

"Well, Laser-Eye, I suppose you owe me for saving you in that pit?"

"Yes, I suppose I do. We will make sure you are well compensated."

"Well then, I think that settles it. I'm all yours Laser-Eye."

"Don't do it, Samuel. You are making a huge mistake."

"Thanks but no thanks, Nige. I think I'll take my chances with

Laser-Eye. He held out both his unmutilated hands for Laser-Eye to shake. Laser-Eye embraced him jovially and vigorously.

"Welcome to the gang, lad."

"You're one of us now," Lionel rasped.

"I am, aren't I?"

A loud bell chimed. Gunthor stood.

"Ah lunchtime, let's go Nige."

"All right, see you later, Nancy." With that they both walked past the killer eyes of Laser-Eye and his gang. Samuel could feel them pierce his soul as they left the infirmary.

"That is not good news."

"No, no it is not. I had hoped better of that Samuel."

They had reached the doors to the canteen now. They left the silence of the corridor and were met by the hustle and bustle of just under 100 four arms eating burgers and chips. They walked to the queue for the food and realised they would be waiting a long time. They waited about five minutes before a fairly new recruit, called Norbert, walked up to them, a grin plastered to his ratty face.

"All right lads, how are you two doing?"

"Fine, Norbert, we're doing just fine."

"Do you guys know what is going on with Seisor? Laser-Eye has been saying some weird stuff."

"Of course he has. Don't listen to him, Norbert. He is an absolute fool. Seisor is the man we fight for. Not him."

"Yeah Nige, you're right. Do you mind if I sit next to you for lunch? No one else likes me. They say I am sickeningly annoying."

"I can't imagine why anyone would say that. Sure you can sit with us, Norbert."

"Yes thanks dudes. You are the nicest guys I know."

They were silent for about ten minutes before they finally arrived at the food. A miserable looking man with a bushy moustache served them each their burgers and a meagre supply of chips. The three men walked over to an empty table and sat down. Nigel went at his burger ravenously. A tall thin four armed man with a beak of a nose and thick spectacles appeared. His name was Silvester.

"Well, chaps, do you mind if I sit here?"

"No, not at all."

"All right, mate. How are you?"

"I'm fine, Norbert. Have you lot heard what that bugger Bagman is saying?"

Theodore Bagman was a highly influential politician who absolutely hated four arms. He was a huge source of hatred for the Armistice. He had been the one responsible for the reduction of four arms to slums. He was the reason why four arms could have no jobs but menial labour.

"No, what has he done this time?"

"He is wanting to set up concentration camps to put us all in."

"He wants to kill us all!"

"It gets worse. He has got some prominent people on his side. Stephen Alan, Pessworth and Gilmour Dagbeth."

"Pissworth and Dogbreath, what do you expect?"

Just then, Laser-Eye walked in, Samuel at his side. He was flanked by seven of his gang members. The queue had dwindled significantly and they made it through in record time. They all congregated on Seisor's table. They were roaring with laughter before long. NIgel stood up to leave. Gunthor followed suit. Silvester and Norbert continued eating. They left to go back to the infirmary so Nigel could collect his things and thank the nurse. They arrived and saw Nancy with her legs on her desk eating a sandwich.

"How are you, Nancy?"

"I'm alright Nige. You?"

"Not good. Samuel seems to have been completely indoctrinated by Laser-Eye."

"Not much you can do about it though."

"No, I guess not."

"It is a shame; he would have been a good addition to our lot."

"That he would, that he would."

With that, Samuel walked in. Alone this time. He limped to his hospital bed and clambered onto it.

"Let's get this operation going then, nurse."

"All right, I'll get the scalpel and the morphine."

"That's good stuff that is."

Nancy returned from the storage cupboard with a syringe and a scalpel as well as a pair of tongs. The needle plunged into Samuel's arm and he smiled a lucid smile. Nancy put on her surgical gloves and prepared for the incision. The scalpel cut into the flesh just above his knee. Nigel spied a glint of metal beneath the gushing of the blood. Nancy put the scalpel down and began attempting to remove the bullet with the tongs. Samuel let out a muffled scream as she dug around inside his leg.

"I've got, I've got it."

There was a soft sucking sound as the bullet was plucked from the flesh. All of a sudden, Nigel heard a sound. A sort of beeping sound. He couldn't make out where it was coming from or if it was just tinnitus. Then he heard it again, slightly louder this time.

"Eh, Gunthor can you hear that?"

"Hear what?"

"That beeping sound."

"What beeping sound?"

Then he saw it. The bullet. It was flashing. A small red LED light was flickering on and off periodically. One beep per flash.

"The bullet, it's flashing."

Nancy wiped the blood off the bullet and sure enough it was flashing.

"What the hell is that?"

It was Nancy who realised.

"It's a tracker!"

Without warning a deafening alarm blared. They could hear the sound of gunfire in the distance. A loud bang. Then more gunfire. They heard frantic footsteps hurtling down the corridor. The door was thrust open. It was Norbert. He was huffing and puffing, his hands on his knees.

"It's the, It's the..."

"What lad, what is it?"

There was another hail of gunfire. Closer this time.

"It's the T.A.I.S, it's the freaking T.A.I.S!"

"Oh..."

To be continued...

Memory photographs

In the photo is my best friend, Leonie, her little sister Kira and me. Directly in front of us in the clear salty water swims a dolphin called Splashy. My family were on a cruise and Antalya was our last stop. I remember it perfectly. The water was blue and the wind was wild. We all wore these terrible safety jackets in light orange. Because of the water all our hair was curly. The dolphin had a light coloured skin, a mixture of grey and blue. His belly was completely white. It was one of those moments when a big dream came true.

– Laura Blumoser

An unusual British day; clear blue sky, warm, yellow midday sun. They stare at you: the deep brown eyes. From such a young and innocent creature exists such a sense of purpose and pride. Standing atop a rough, grey boulder, which he undoubtably had been put on, was Woozle. The young pup, frozen in time, forever young. Where has his sense of adventure gone? The rag-tag puppy had enjoyed the wilderness, feeling the bitter English wind flow through his fur. We'll never forget what he was like, even if he does.

– Corbin Shearing

Two ordinary people with no care in the world. Both slouching nonchalantly, trying their best not to break character. One wraps their arm around with a familiarity born of a time long gone yet one so warming to the touch. This photo marks the beginning of something new and meaningful, a budding flower, so bright in the Spring.

– Isaac Atkinson

It is a still moment in time. The photo is of a bunch of the hockey team in mid fall. It is like a domino effect. Faces are all unposed to reveal a natural emotion. When I see it now, I can't help but laugh. It is a perfect moment in time where everyone was humble, united, not just by our same uniform, but in spirit and camaraderie. Although after that we went into bickering on the field, at that moment the photo shows when everything was perfect, in the middle of a fall, that captures the pure essence of fun and of the love we had for each other.

– Anna-Luisa Ayckbourn

I Come From...

I come from falling asleep in Church, stealing wine out the cupboard and Skypes with my dad every other Sunday.

I come from YouTube binges and smashed controllers, making friends whose names and faces I didn't know.

I come from a family that never ends, houses all over the world but no money.

I come from drivers who stole gas money, beggars lining every street and a country with oil and crops but no electricity or food.

I come from losing faith, screaming into pillows, crying in locked bathrooms and burns and cuts on my arms and chest.

I come from a strong dislike of Capitalism, a love of guns and snakes that turned to a love of superheroes and rap music.

I come from heat hazes and traffic that really never ever moved.

I come from an accent I picked up from TV and just never dropped, from always being a year too young.

I come from lying, all the time, about things that really didn't matter.

I come from taking the internet way too seriously.

– Damilare Williams-Shires

I come from a dirt town with flowerbeds around every corner.

From the salty smell of the fresh sea breeze

And strong winds which pushed me to play in the sand.

I come from a building tall enough to touch the sky

But small enough to make me feel safe.

I come from the sounds of samba music playing

The sounds of laughter and happiness.

I come from applause and praise

But also judgement and hate.

I come from a house of two languages

Both creating a familiar harmony which keeps my head clear.

I come from a place of pressure

A place of worrying where I'll go and what I will do.

I come from a place of love.

– Anna-Luisa Ayckbourn

I come from fluffed up pillows,

Shiny radiators,

Sweet chocolate and luscious hair.

I come from sandy castles,

Sun block,

Skateboarding and bike locks.

I come from plastic blocks,

Hard backed books,

Bright blue crocs and shady looks.

I come from comics and games,

Sun and rain

Dirt covered parks and muddy ramps.

– Henry Atkinson

I come from the stench of seaweed
And sand between my toes,
The crashing waves and searching for firewood
Crowded streets to barren fields.

I come from the seagull's screech,
The empty graveyard and the pew with no cushion.
The warmth of soup filling my stomach
And the chill of ice cream on the front.

– Isaac Atkinson

I come from hot, from sea and from sun
From mirrors with the same picture for all.
I come from dolls, imagination and games
From humour, comprehension and laughs.
I come from making everyone feel good
But by confusing myself
I come from different people and different places.
I come from changes.

– Nuria Escoda

I come from two outdoor toilets
At the bottom of the garden.
Learning which way cars drive
From looking out of the window.

I come from sick on my carseat
And saving weeks for a Doctor Who figure.
Catherine wheels on monkey trees
And hosing down grandma.

I come from Tonka Toys in my quarry
And eczema from limpets
I come from child neighbours behind fireplaces
And moisturiser tub drumkits.

– Asa Jones

I come from a city that stretches for miles across the land
Filled with fancy cars and gigantic clocks.
I come from mistakes and misfortunes that reformed me
From the fish and chip shop heading towards the hospital
I have cracked my head open all the way down to my skull.
I come from a small town filled with familiar faces
And graffiti saying "Kilroy was here."
I come from tutoring over equations that have depressed me
And made my life even more difficult.

– Silas Venus-Haslett

I come from the night garden and Iggle Piggle
From the first day at preschool where I was lost.
I come from Hallowe'en and all the scary faces
Some with masks and some with none.

I come from Essex and the homeless
Who are sleeping.
From climbing trees and walking on the beach.

– Toby Richardson

I come from a hospital full of nurses wearing pink and just pink.
With cloudy visions and voices and cries.
From endless buildings with eyes like flies and mouths
Wide open waiting for children.

I come from cats rubbing themselves on my leg leaving orange fur
everywhere.
From laughing at the man trying to pick up my mom
From night and morning of maths homework
Piled up because of laziness

I come from making holes in walls with my pen which will forever
be secret.

– Hee Joo Jin

I come from dark nights, wet roads and bright lights
From plane rides and long bike rides
I come from boredom and chores
The dried crack a few streets away
The Sun reflecting off the concrete.
I come from playing gamecube with my brother
From fist fights and Lego
From California on Hallowe'en.

– Kieran Smith

I come from a small stable directly before the Alps

It was terrible weather the first weekend.

I was important.

I helped with the ponies.

I was friendly and polite.

I ate all from my plate.

They said I was friendly and polite the whole weekend.

They said 10 o'clock lights was out

So I turned off my light at exactly 10 o'clock.

I never came late and do all they want of me.

As we drove away I was crying.

But a month later I went back.

But nobody remembered my name.

– Laura Blumoser

I come from the dinner of broccoli
Where I snuck some on my brother's plate.
I come from the pain of that time
When I split my knee open on the trampoline.

I come from that stinky old car
With the rope on the floor
And something growing out of it.

I come from the play school with all those people
Who always look happy but are probably bored.

I come from all those people looking up at me.
I come from that time I set a pillow on fire
Using a piece of grass from the fire pit.

I come from the toyshop
Because I wanted to.

– Damon Kelly

I come from a courtroom

From falling through a barbed wire fence.

I come from shooting

Dog walking

Dead rats

Dumb ideas.

I come from blowing things up.

– Alan Davison

I come from toy cars and Lego bricks

From made top games which I thought were real.

From old friends and good friends

And paths which never end

And rubbish birthdays.

I come from a bicycle crash

From new things and dog walks

From good looks and chased dreams

– Freddie Elson

I come from stuff and things
Under the tunnel with Thomas
But never sleeping alone.
The darkness coming
But never reaching I dreamt ahead.

I come from my home,
Whichever I remember
Empty streets, barking dogs
A school now forgotten.
I built my streets from red and yellow,
Yet never did I walk there.

I come from two brothers
No room, pitiful squabbles,
The backseat, never old enough for the front,
Late night travels and sleeping in the car
Awake to orange lights

I come from the woods
The dog pack and I
The Queen's master
Running from the shadow.

– Corbin Shearing

Fyling Hall School is a mixed, small, independent day and boarding school set in the North York Moors National Park, with magnificent views over Robin Hood's Bay.

It offers excellent teaching with some of the best results and added value in the county, in small class sizes from foundation, primary, through GCSE to A Level.

The school has comprehensive facilities
including an indoor and open-air
theatre, a sports hall and climbing wall,
an all-weather pitch, athletics ground
and riding school.

Fyling Hall School, Robin Hood's Bay,
North Yorkshire YO22 4QD

01947 880353 / 00 44 (0)1947 880353

office@fylinghall.org

www.fylinghall.org

 FYLING HALL SCHOOL